THE TIMEWEAVER'S WAGER

AXEL BLACKWELL

CHAPTER 1

GLEN MCCLAY SAT ON A fallen tree beside the dead girl's shrine, staring down the train tracks to the point in the distance where the two rails converged. In the summer, the sun's heat conjured shimmering mirages at that focal point. Glen would pretend the mirage was Connie's ghost coming to visit him. He could sit and watch her for hours, had done so, in fact, on several occasions. It was good to see her walking toward him. Maybe she wanted to see him again. Maybe she had forgiven him, or at least was willing to try. But it was also good that she never actually reached him. Glen didn't want her to see what he had become, or rather, what he had failed to become.

There would be no mirage today. Summer was gone. It was late October and the sun had lost its strength to bend the fringes of reality. The tracks stretched toward the horizon, dwindling to a hard, sharp point. The ghost was gone, as was the girl, as were the eight years of Glen's life since her death.

He looked the other direction. Holman Avenue crossed the tracks a stone's throw to his left. Beyond that, the rail line hooked a right and disappeared behind a stand of hardwood timber. His pickup truck waited on the shoulder near the crossing arm. As he watched, Alan Fontain's glossy black Lincoln parked behind his Ford.

Glen pulled a grim smile and turned his attention to his hands. They were pale and thin and sounded papery as he wrung them together. Beneath them, his sneakers rested on black-and-white flecked chunks of granite. The Lincoln's door opened, then a moment later closed quietly. Alan's leather-soled shoes tapped across the asphalt, then crunched in the gravel between the road and Connie's shrine.

Glen continued looking down at his hands until Alan's shoes, as black as his town car, appeared in Glen's field of vision. Alan placed a gloved hand on his shoulder, letting it settle briefly before giving a gentle squeeze. Glen did not lift his head. He turned his hands palms up, spreading his fingers.

Alan spoke. "Did you see her today?" His voice was smooth, endowed with a quiet power. Glen loved that voice, in an odd and awkward way. It calmed him, centered him, drew him away from his despair.

"No," Glen said, glancing again down the iron

rails.

"How long have you been here?"

"Not that long, I don't think." But even as he said this he noticed his butt had gone numb and the flesh under his nails had gone blue from the cold. Just how long had he been sitting here?

"Mary Beth called, worried about you," Alan said with a chuckle that almost didn't sound forced. "She, uh, she usually doesn't call unless you've been gone a while."

"I didn't walk out, Alan," Glen said. "I made arrangements. Billie's covering Aikido and women's self-defense. Charlotte's got Neighborhood Watch and Fiona has the call center."

"It's not The Project I'm worried about." Alan patted his shoulder. "It's cold out here, bud. You want to go grab some coffee?"

Glen chuckled, though he didn't smile. It was an old joke between them. "If it tasted as good as it smelled..." he said.

"I swear, Glen, before I'm through with you, you will learn to love coffee."

"I guess it's gonna be a while before you're through with me, then," he said, and finally looked up at Alan.

"Let us hope so, my boy, let us hope," Alan said. Glen had been a boy when they first met, seven years ago, but he was twenty-three now. Alan might have been forty, but had the aura of a much older man. His hair was black, silvering at the temples. His face was that of a Roman Emperor, with eyes as bright as blue diamonds. "But if you keep sitting out here in this cold, you'll catch your death. Can you at least tell me you'll get out of the weather for the rest of the evening?"

"Yeah," Glen said, raising slowly to his feet. Blood coursed oddly through his stiff legs. Feeling tingled its way back into his numb butt. "What time is it, anyway?"

Alan's smile faded. "It's nearly six," he said.

Glen grimaced, troubled but not surprised. In the eight years since Connie's death, he had been coming here from time to time, hoping to catch a glimpse of her ghost, hoping to finally learn how to confront the remorse and shame that had become the core of his existence. But this year, it was different. He had visited the shrine several times a week since summer, staying longer as the days grew shorter. Losing time. A break was coming, an end of some sort. This business – the business of Constance Salvatore and these iron rails and the boy who left her to die – must be resolved before fall gave way to winter, or it would never be resolved at all.

"I'm sorry about today..." Glen started, but a slight wrinkling of Alan's brow silenced him.

"The girls can handle The Project for a day." Alan's eyes pinned Glen in place. He wanted to look away, but couldn't. "Maybe they'd be okay for a week without you. But, Glen, *you* are The Project. You are the *heart* of this thing. You understand that, right?"

Glen turned his body (though he still couldn't look away from Alan's eyes) and gestured toward the tracks, as if Connie were standing there now.

Alan grimaced, then wrapped an arm around Glen's shoulder. He pulled him in for a tight one-armed hug, then guided him toward their vehicles. "Connie is the inspiration, the motivation, the mascot. But you, my boy, are the one who makes things happen. She may be the spirit of this thing, but you are its body. You are the one doing the work. And if we want to keep the work going," he paused, pointing to Glen as they walked, "we've got to keep you going. Right?"

Glen nodded. He trudged along beside Alan, his shoes crunching through the chunks of granite underlying the railway. "I think maybe her spirit has moved on. Like, maybe she just gave up on us and drifted away."

Alan didn't respond. Glen assumed that the state of Connie's spirit wasn't all that relevant to Alan, though neither would ever say such a thing. Glen guessed Alan wasn't the type to believe in spirits.

"Did you know, we could read each other's minds?" Glen said.

"Really?" Alan asked.

"Not all the time," Glen said, "but enough to freak out our parents. When I was twelve, I stepped on a nail. The thing went halfway through my foot. Connie was there waiting for us at the emergency room. She had ridden her bike because she knew I was hurt and was worried about me. Nobody told her, she just knew. And I knew sometimes, too...like what she named her new kitten before she told me, or what grade she got on her math final.

"And then after she...after she was gone, it was like there was a place in my mind that was empty. Like a blank spot, you know, where part of her mind used to be. When I came here, though, I could still feel some sort of connection, or an echo, or something. But now, I just don't know. It's like she's slipping away."

Alan tightened his arm around Glen's shoulder. They walked together along the rails, Alan's long wool coat swished against his legs. A breeze picked up, cutting through Glen's jeans and light jacket. As they neared the avenue, the rails began to hum, infused with the energy of cargo and box cars thundering through the Midwestern countryside.

Alan looked down the tracks. "How long have we got?"

"Three minutes, tops," Glen said.

"God, that fast? I can't even see it yet."

Glen nodded. Somewhere down the line, a whistle

cried, distant but impending.

They reached their vehicles. Glen climbed into his truck, but Alan stopped him before he could close the door. "I'll make you an offer – how about you take tomorrow off," he said. "I mean, don't show up at The Project, and for God's sake, don't show up here." He paused. "I need you to be sharp at the gala tomorrow night."

"About that..." Glen started.

"Glen." Alan lowered his head, just a little. One eye narrowed. "These events are where the real work gets done. It's how we keep Connie's memory alive, not just in your heart, but in the hearts of every member of this community. This is how we protect our community, how we stop what happened to Connie from happening to anyone else. And those donors are showing up to see you just as much as they are to see me."

"I know, Alan, I get that."

"And so you also get that this is a favor we owe Mayor Anderson, this event could help change his title to Senator Anderson. If all goes well, The Project will be in a position to owe him many more favors in the future, right?"

"I know, but we need to talk..." Glen said, groping for words.

"Train's coming, Glen," Alan said. Its whistle blasted again, loud enough to make conversation difficult. Alan raised his voice. "Be there, be sharp. If we need to talk, I promise to make time for you afterward. Understand?"

Glen nodded once more. He understood. He would do as Alan asked, just like he always had. Just like he always would.

CHAPTER 2

GLEN PULLED INTO HIS SISTER'S driveway as the sun set. He hit the clicker and waited for the garage door to roll up. There had once been a stairway at the back of the garage leading up to an apartment, but his sister, Sophia, had removed all the risers and boarded that door.

"You need a place with someone around to look after you," she had told him in her smoke-hardened voice, "and I have a place. You can live in the loft over my garage as long as you like, but you *will* stop in and say 'hi' when you come and go. That's the deal."

Glen figured she regretted that stipulation as much as he did – most of the time, anyway. But they both knew it was right, necessary, and so the deal remained. To reach his apartment, he would have to walk through her kitchen to a set of interior stairs.

He had hoped she would be out tonight – he had overheard her on the phone, making plans with someone — but the lights were on inside, and her car was parked in the other garage bay. He slipped quietly into the house. A pink sticky note from the door frame snagged on his shirt, then fluttered to the floor. *Turn off oven.* He replaced it on the frame with several other of Sophia's reminders. Warm yellow light and the smell of cooling home-cooked dinner filled the kitchen. Below that aroma hung the pervasive odor of cigarette smoke.

Blue television light glowed from the otherwise darkened living room. Electronic laughter and *beeps* and *boops* droned out of some game show or other on the tube. "There's some leftover casserole for you in the fridge," Sophia called from the other room.

"Not hungry...thanks though," Glen said, doing his best to sound cheerful, or at least alive.

The couch creaked, and the television snapped off. "Glen," she called again.

"I'm fine, sis," he said. "I just...I've got work, you know, papers and stuff." He made a vague gesture toward his apartment.

She appeared between kitchen and living room, leaning against the inside of the archway. The scar across her forehead peaked out below her bangs as she scrutinized him with narrowed eyes. A grey cat, Smoke they called him, twined a figure-eight around her ankles, gave Glen a dismissive look, then vanished back into the darkened living room.

Sophia thrust a smoldering cigarette at the refrigerator. "Glen. Eat the damn casserole, you're so skinny I can see through you."

"I said, I'm not hungry." He rubbed his temple. "You're missing your show."

"I saw the news, earlier. Guess who was on TV again?," she asked. Her left eye sometimes drifted up and off to the side, but not now. At this moment, both eyes glared at him.

Glen made no reply.

"You're a goddamn hero, Glen. Some little girl in Topeka, Kansas did CPR on her baby brother. She said she learned it at one of your classes." Sophia raised her cigarette to her lips, took a long drag, then let the hand holding it hang straight down. Smoke rolled slowly out of her nostrils. "Topeka, Kansas for Christ's sake."

"So, what do you want me to do about it?" Glen shrugged, inching toward the stairs.

"Take some fucking credit! That's what I want you to do, like you used to. Stop moping around here like a damn zombie..."

They both knew the rest of everything that came after this line. She had told him enough times already. Everybody had. To say it again would make the lines even emptier than they already were. *It's not your fault. There wasn't anything you could have done. You can't blame yourself, yadda yadda yadda ad infinitum.*

He stared at her, no longer trying to project a lifelike appearance, his eyes as dead as he could make them. They both knew his lines, too. *You don't understand. You didn't know her like I did. You don't know what happened that night.*

"You see any ghosts today?" she asked, casually, after several seconds.

Glen shook his head.

"Connie has moved on, hasn't she?" There was no anger in her voice at the moment. Glen admired her tenacity, and her self control. "You said so yourself."

"Yeah, I guess so," he said, letting his guard down just a bit. "Maybe she has, or maybe she's about to."

"Well, maybe you need to grow up and move on, too," Sophia snapped. "Instead of wallowing around this dump, mooning over some grade-school girlfriend who's been dead eight years. All while you've got fifty women who'd take you right now if you could pull your head out of your ass and acknowledge them.

"Any man who gets up on stage beside Alan Fontain has his pick of women around here – with your fancy tux, with all that glitz and glam and glitter. And Money. Fuck, *I'd* almost sleep with you if you weren't such a self-obsessed asshole," then, as an afterthought she added, "and if you weren't my brother."

He started to say, *Dale might have a problem with that,* but he saw tears seeping into her lower lids and thought

14

better of it. "I've been thinking a little about Rochelle," he said, "maybe we could try again..."

Sophia scoffed, loudly, and turned away. "What happened, Glen? You were doing better. Things were going to be okay."

And just what was he supposed to say to that? That things were never going to be okay? That Connie was slipping away, was moving on, and once she did he would lose his chance to right his wrongs? That Connie wasn't moving on because she had found peace but because she had finally given up on him?

What happened was simple. He had poured his guilt and grief, and love maybe, yes maybe even his love, into The Constance Salvatore Project. He had fooled himself into believing that by saving lives and fighting crime in her name he could somehow make up for what had happened that night. And as long as he had held her memory sharp and vivid in his mind, as long as he flogged himself with the tasks and speeches and classes and civic duty of it all, it had worked, kind of. He had been able to ignore that awful hateful voice in the back of his head telling him he let her die.

But now, her ghost was gone, her memory was faded. The Project had made him a celebrity, of sorts, and it had been turned into a political trophy for whatever politician could lay claim to any piece of the apparatus. And Connie was still dead. And he was still the coward who had run away and let it happen. And he was still the liar who had helped cover it up.

He looked up at Sophia. She thrust both arms down, palms up and gave him her most exasperated WTF look. "Would you just eat the goddamn casserole?" she said, finally. "Could you at least do that for your poor sister?"

"I'm going to bed, Sophia." He turned and went up the stairs before she could say more.

CHAPTER 3

GLEN LAY AWAKE STARING AT the ceiling as he did most nights. One advantage to living with Sophia was she took his mind off Connie from time to time. If one sorrow failed to torment him sufficiently, he had a second to fall back on.

Sophia had graduated as a Registered Nurse and was half way through her hospital internship on the night Connie died. A month or two after Connie's death, Sophia had been involved in a terrible auto wreck. Glen didn't remember many details, that whole year was cloaked in a fog of grief and misery.

She sustained a traumatic brain injury in the crash and was comatose for several days. After she awoke, she had suffered seizures. The doctors managed to control these with medication, but other problems persisted. She could not read for more than a few minutes without triggering a migraine, and her short term memory was shot.

Her pleasant personality and gentle spirit had won her many friends during the short time she interned at the hospital. The administrators wanted to keep her on, but an RN with a faulty memory just doesn't work. They put her internship "on hold," until her condition improved, though her doctors said that wasn't likely. When the doctors cleared her to return to work, the hospital found a place for her in housekeeping. Between that and the insurance money, Sophia had managed to establish an independent life for herself.

Her biggest long-term problem was her memory. Some days it worked just fine, other days...not so much. Once, she used up an entire month's worth of cell minutes in a single call. She phoned Cineplex Odeon to check movie times, found she and Dale had just enough time to get to Matrix Reloaded if she hurried, and rushed out the door. She forgot to take her cell phone, and forgot to hit *end*. The recorded movie times repeated their loop for nearly four hours. It probably would have gone on another twelve (she ended up at Dale's house that night) except the battery finally died.

Other forgetfulness episodes had been less innocuous. Shortly after Glen moved into the apartment, Sophia started to fill the tub, realized she was out of wine, and left for the market. Glen arrived home in time to turn the water off before more than the bathroom and hall flooded.

She used to burn food. Frequently. Dale bought her an IPhone one Christmas and programed a series of apps, timers, reminders, and lists that helped her keep life on track and moving forward. There were also reminders on checklists and sticky notes at both the front and back doors.

Glen had taken the apartment above the garage as much to look out for her as to have her looking out for him, but he'd never dare suggest that. Sophia had fought hard to win back her life after the accident. Any suggestion that she needed help would be seen not only as an insult but also as a threat to her future independence.

CHAPTER 4

SOMETIME AFTER ELEVEN O'CLOCK, GLEN slipped into the kitchen and reheated the casserole. He thought he had heard Dale's old Honda pull into Sophia's drive, but he didn't hear it leave. The living room was dark, the TV off. Glen used a paper plate so Sophia wouldn't hear dishes clinking, and he stopped the microwave before it dinged. Maybe Dale had decided to spend the night. Glen hoped so. He felt bad for upsetting Sophia. If she had a good man in her bed, she wouldn't be laying awake worrying about her damaged brother. And Dale was a good man, as good as Sophia was likely to find.

He ate his meal in the dark. Chicken and bacon and potatoes in some sort of cream sauce. It was probably delicious, but Glen didn't notice. It had been eight years since Connie's death, but not eight years of this. The first year had been hard, terrible in fact. But then he turned sixteen, got a job, got a car, started The

Project.

The Project had fixed everything, gave him an outlet for his grief and a foil for his guilt. Life had returned to a sane state of relative goodness. There was still that empty spot in his head, and a gaping hole in his heart, but those are the types of wounds every person acquires on their trip from childhood to old-age, the types of wounds that are incorporated into a life's story rather than defining an entire existence.

But somewhere along the way, things changed. The Project had been the cure to Glen's devastation, but the cure wasn't taking. It had pushed back the tide of sorrow and blunted the poison needle of guilt. But the guilt was still there, buried deep and leaking. And the tide of sorrow? Well, no one can holdback the tide forever. The Project was like an organ that had been transplanted into Glen's life to replace some vital part of him that had perished, but now he was rejecting the organ. That's what it was, wasn't it? The Project itself was poisoning him. Or was that just what his sister wanted him to believe? He didn't know. It was late. He was tired.

He slid a second paper plate out of the cabinet and wrote neatly in magic marker across its back,

Thank you Sophia
it was delicious
I love you

21

Glen

He looked at the plate for a moment, then crumpled it up with his dirty one and stuffed them both in the trash can. Halfway up the stairs to his apartment, he stopped, went back down to the kitchen, and rewrote the note on a third plate. This time he drew what he hoped was a silly-cute smiley face beside the text. He almost added, *sorry I'm an asshole,* but didn't. He left the plate leaning against her coffee pot, then went to bed.

CHAPTER 5

THAT NIGHT HE DREAMED. It was a memory of the last time he had ever known what was going on inside Connie's mind. He was her, was actually inside her head in the dream, as she lay under the pale summer moon, broken beyond repair. Blood bubbled in her nostrils when she tried to breathe. Blood in her mouth, in her throat. She choked on it. Her mind was full of a hurt she didn't understand, and an empty confused bewilderment. Her clothing clung to the thick and sticky blood that seemed to be everywhere. And that was odd – that she was clothed – hadn't they taken her clothing? She didn't want to remember. She tried to move, but couldn't manage much. Her limbs felt as if they had been severed, attached now only by thin ribbons of pain. She rolled to one side on the lumpy, no – on the *rocky* ground, and dragged an arm in front of her. Her hand fell onto something cold – a rail, an iron rail, thrumming with energy. Somewhere very close, a train whistle screamed.

CHAPTER 6

ROSALIE PARKED HER HOME MAID hatchback in the pebble-paved roundabout and smiled. Alan Fontain was her favorite client. For one thing, she was paid hourly, and at least half the hours she spent at Alan's were in conversation with the man, rather than actually working. For another thing, he was an excellent conversationalist. He paid close attention to her when she talked, making her feel comfortable despite her difficulty with the language. He complimented often and always seemed able to make her smile, not that Rosalie ever found smiling difficult. He remembered the names of her four children and seven grandchildren. He usually remembered their birthdays as well, though Rosalie suspected he had a computer remind him of those dates.

And, he tipped better than her hourly wage.

She let herself in through the front door with a key he had provided, and punched the maid's code into the security panel. Speakers throughout the house emitted a pleasant series of tones, announcing her presence. Sometimes, Alan would call out a merry welcome, but today there was no answer to the chimes. That was good, she thought, good that he slept in sometimes. He was such a busy man, a good man. And, though she thoroughly enjoyed his company, there was work that just didn't get done if he was there talking to her all morning. She quickly compiled a mental list of things to do before he awoke.

Her smile faltered. Something was off about the house. She stood very still, listening, but the house was quiet. She hung her coat on one of the many hooks by the door, then stepped into the central hall. Here, a broad staircase swooped in a graceful arc to the right, meeting an open walkway on the second floor. A smell hung in the air, very faint but acrid. Rosalie sniffed, looked around, sniffed. *Smoke?* Maybe Alan had burnt toast? But, no, it wasn't toast, maybe stew burnt to the bottom of a pan? What had he been up to? Rosalie rolled her eyes. Whatever he had done, she hoped he hadn't tried to clean it up himself. Or hide it. "Ay!" she muttered to herself. Men could be such children sometimes. She put her to do list on hold in favor of checking the kitchen for charcoal crusted cookery or other disasters.

Rosalie whistled an improvised tune as she did her

inspection. Nothing in the kitchen or dining area suggested a culinary disaster. Maybe he had burned a bag of microwave popcorn, then thrown it in the outside garbage to avoid any additional burnt odor in the house. She supposed that was possible, but it still concerned her. A properly cleaned home should *smell* clean, and the homes Rosalie cleaned were cleaned proper.

She sniffed the air again. There was no mess in the kitchen, which was good, but if something had burned elsewhere in the house, that could be much worse. The odor was very faint now. Which struck Rosalie as odd. Why had it dissipated so quickly? And another odd thing, it now smelled more like gasoline than burnt stew. Maybe there had been an electrical fire during the night? Houses these days were full of little electrical things, just everywhere you looked. Anyone of those things may have shorted out, burnt up.

The idea that there had been an electrical fire lodged itself in her head, even though the burnt odor was nearly undetectable now. A whole house inspection was in order. She moved quickly from room to room, sampling the air like a surfacing prairie dog, and sweeping the wall sockets with her eyes. She searched the kitchen, dining room, breakfast room, nibble nook, pantry, and atrium without finding anything amiss. The formal living room, sitting room, and billiards room were all in order.

It was in Alan's office that she first noticed the footprints. All the other rooms she had inspected thus far either had hardwood or marble flooring. The floor of Alan's office, however, was covered in a lush burgundy carpet, so thick it would tickle your ankles. This carpet displayed, very clearly, the crisp elongated triangle pattern Rosalie had laid down last time she vacuumed. That had been two days ago.

Alan's footprints were visible, traveling from the door to his desk and back. One set of prints indicated a journey from his desk to the bay window overlooking his gardens. There was nothing unusual about these tracks. What caught Rosalie's eye were the other tracks. Something else had also walked through this room since its last vacuuming, leaving a bizarre heart-shaped mark. Rosalie studied the marks for over minute before realizing what had made them – a pair of women's shoes, with a heel so high and sharp, its pencil-thin point was only an inch behind the tiny triangle of its toe.

Rosalie frowned. What kind of woman wears a shoe like that? The word *naca* came into her mind. She shoved that aside, scolding herself. Was it any of her business? No, of course not. But still, how could a woman even stand up in a shoe like that, let alone walk.

Perhaps Alan hadn't come down this morning, she

thought, because he had a lady friend upstairs with him. That happened from time to time, which also was none of Rosalie's business. Each time in the past, when he had had company, the lady's coat would be hanging on the rack in the foyer. This had been the signal that he was to be undisturbed – to prevent embarrassing either of them. But there had been no coat on the rack other than her own. Also, if he did have a lady friend spend the night with him, one who wore heels taller than Rosalie's whole foot, why had she walked a circle around his office? Maybe he had given her a tour of his house? That didn't sound like Alan at all.

The only other carpeted room on this floor was the library/conservatory. It lay at the opposite end of the house. Rosalie quickly padded back through the halls on her flat, sensible shoes. They were silent over the hardwoods and marble. She pushed open the double doors, revealing a room full of leather and mahogany, and an entire forest worth of books. At the far end, a baby grand sat before a curved bank of floor-to-ceiling windows.

The carpet and lighting in this room revealed the tracks in even finer detail. Rosalie traced their path without entering the room. The mystery woman had meandered from one stack of books to the next, pausing to sit in each of the four wingback chairs, before settling in at the piano bench. From there to the green marble fireplace, and then back out through these doors.

Rosalie shuddered. Two things struck her as very, very wrong – in addition to the fact that only a whore would wear shoes like that, not that it was any of her business. First, Alan's footprints did not accompany the woman's. He had not been in this room since Rosalie last vacuumed. Second, and somehow much worse, there was another set of prints here – tiny, barefoot footprints, the kind only a toddler could make.

She stood for a moment, irresolute. She hadn't liked the look of the stiletto prints, but the toddler prints unsettled her even more. Why, she could not say. The whole situation felt incredibly spooky. Why would some hooker and her barefoot baby be wandering around in Alan's house with out him?

Rosalie had long ago learned that action cures fear. The action she wanted to take was to go ask Alan if everything was okay. But if she did that, and if the woman was in his bed, well, that would just be bad for everybody. But those tracks – Rosalie decided it would be better for everybody if those tracks were not there.

With no further consideration, she went into action. A closet just outside the library contained a coiled vacuum hose. Rosalie grabbed this and plugged it into the central vac socket in the library's wall. Somewhere in the guts of the house, the powerful vacuum unit whirred to life and the hose whooshed. In less than ten minutes, not one footprint remained. When she finished, she could no longer smell anything other than leather, wood, and paper.

She re-coiled the hose in its closet, padded back to the office, pulled a vacuum hose from a closet there, and sucked up any footprints that may or may not have been left in the office carpet.

Rosalie wasn't angry, not really. Alan had many fine lady friends. Sometimes they stayed the night. There was nothing wrong with that, she supposed. His little indiscretions were harmless, and his good deeds more than made up for any character flaws. He was, after all, a bachelor, and he never put on any airs of holiness. She would say a prayer for him tonight, and light a candle. Or maybe two.

But why had there been a baby in the house? Rosalie frowned again. Perhaps she *should* wake Alan, just to check on him. She looked at the sweeping staircase. No sounds drifted down from above. Did Alan have company? She looked to the coat rack in the entry way. Her coat hung there alone. It was much too cold to be out and about without a coat, even for a tramp in eight-inch stilettos. She looked back to the staircase, and after another moment's hesitation, she began to climb.

CHAPTER 7

GLEN HAD INTENDED TO DO exactly as Alan directed. Taking a day off from The Project would normally be the worst thing for his mental health, but maybe it was time to move on. Maybe a day or two away could help him come to grips with his life and his future.

The October morning was clear and cold. Glen inhaled the crisp air and surveyed his sister's back yard. A raised section near the back fence had once been a garden but had long since gone to dandelions and thistles. The skeletal remains of last years prickly crop stood as black silhouettes against the cedar fence. Glen thought maybe today would be a good day to till the weeds under. Perhaps this was a year for planting in ground long left fallow.

He found a pair of rough leather gloves and a shovel in the garage. Rubber boots would have been nice, but Sophia's were several sizes too small. He wore his old sneakers instead. They were soaked with dew before he got half way across the yard. By the time he had turned over the third shovel-full of soil, the shoes, socks and jeans' cuffs were black with mud. He figured he'd be caked with the stuff before the job was done.

As he finished the first row, his cell phone rang. It took him several seconds to get his gloves off, fish the phone out of his pocket, and hit *answer*. By that time, the call had gone to voice mail, but there was no need to wait for the message. The caller ID displayed *Alan Fontain Home*.

Glen stared at the phone in his dirty hand. He had just started to work up a sweat, was just getting into the job. If he called Alan back now, he might as well give up on accomplishing anything else for the rest of the day. The last thing he wanted was for Sophia to come home and see that he had started this little project, only to abandon it part-way through.

Before he had a chance to decide whether he should return the call, the phone rang again. Glen frowned, staring at *Alan Fontain Home* on the readout. Alan did not call twice. He didn't do anything twice. If he did it once, it was done. A message left was the end of the matter. Despite this, the phone continued to ring. Glen hit *Answer*.

The voice on the other end was not Alan. Glen felt a weird disconnect somewhere between his ears and his brain. Instead of the calm, smooth voice he had expected, the caller was whispering fast, desperate, near hysteria. It was a woman, Glen realized, a foreign woman, speaking in a foreign language – or with an accent too strange to decipher. His mind raced to catch up with the stream of words pouring out of his telephone.

"Wait," he said, "slow down, I can't understand...Who is this?"

"Glen, I tell you, I start over. I think you need to come right away," the voice rattled at him. "It's Alan, I think something happen. I think he's not okay."

"Rosalie?" Glen asked. "Is that you? What's wrong with Alan? Does he need an ambulance?"

"No, no, no ambulance. Yes it's me, who else? You need to come. He's...there's something wrong. He is crying. He is just sitting and staring at the wall and I don't know what to do."

Glen knew Rosalie well. At Alan's insistence, she had attended self-defense and CPR classes sponsored by The Project. All of Alan's employees had. Glen had instructed her CPR class and had participated in several Aikido sessions with her. She was generally a well-grounded, level-headed woman. Her current panic unnerved him.

"Rosalie, breathe. Take a breath. Tell me what happened."

"Nothing," she whispered, nearly pleading, "nothing happen. I just come in to do the carpet and he is sitting on the floor talking to the wall and crying and he won't look at me."

"Okay," Glen said. He looked down at his mud caked shoes and pant legs. "Okay, listen, it will take me a couple of minutes, but I will..."

In the background, on Rosalie's end of the line, Glen heard Alan's voice, "Rosalie." She gasped. Alan continued, "That will be enough of that, Rosalie." He sounded like a father scolding a two-year-old for interrupting while adults are talking.

She quickly whispered, "I have to go. Please come." Then the line went dead.

Glen stripped off his muddy clothes and left them in the garage. Sophia would bitch, but what else was new? He threw on the first clean clothes he found and headed for Alan's.

CHAPTER 8

TWENTY-FIVE MINUTES LATER, HE was banging on the door of Alan's mansion. Rosalie's car was nowhere to be seen. Alan answered the door dressed in a precisely tailored white button-down shirt, open at the collar, and slacks that probably cost more than Glen spent on a week's worth of meals. He smiled his broad, indulgent smile, eyes crinkling at the corners. His air was that of a man completely in control, not only of himself but also of everything he touched. *In other words,* Glen thought, *exactly as he has always been.*

"Glen, come in," he said warmly, almost apologetically. He led Glen into the foyer, but they went no further. On a typical visit, they would have retired to the sunny breakfast room at the back of the house to discuss life or business, but this was not a typical visit. For one thing, there was the smell – charred meat, gasoline maybe – faint but noticeable. There was something else, too, about Alan. Glen couldn't immediately identify the problem, but something was wrong.

"Hey, Alan," he said, "are you alright? It smells like smoke in here."

Then Glen saw it, just a flickering waver in Alan's demeanor, maybe, but Glen caught a glimpse of a truth he had always known but never dared admit – Alan was *not* a minor god after all. Something had disturbed his unfaltering self-possession. Alan controlled every molecule within his sphere. He did now, as he always had, but subtle lines in his face betrayed this serene façade. He had been scared, scared badly, and not so long ago.

This realization showed on Glen's face before he had a chance to suppress it. Alan's indulgent smile turned cheerily dismissive almost immediately. He shook his head, "Not at all, Glen, it's nothing, really. So sorry to drag you all the way out here on your day off. Rosalie is a sweet lady, a lovely lady, and very good at her work, but she does have a flair for drama. I assure you I'll be fine. I am feeling a bit out of sorts this morning – strange dreams, stranger wakings. Nothing that I remember, but...I think it's this house. This house might be, I don't know, too *big* for me, maybe?"

The house was indeed enormous. One of the many companies Alan owned was a construction firm specializing in high-end custom homes. This wasn't their largest project ever, but it wasn't their smallest, either.

"Where is Rosalie?" Glen asked.

"I sent her home."

"Is she okay?"

Alan seemed taken aback. "Of course she's okay. Why wouldn't she be?"

"She just seemed really upset.'

Alan chuckled lightly, an easy, calming sound. "I guess she was," he said. "I must have given her quite a scare."

"And what about you?" Glen asked. "Don't tell me you're just fine..."

"I am fine, Glen."

"No, something happened – I've known you most of my life - I can tell just by looking at you. And Rosalie was scared, not just worried, *scared*. That's not like her. You know that."

"Enough," Alan said, holding up a hand. "I am trying really hard to be okay. I have things to do today, important things, but you and Rosalie insist on blowing my cover." He shook his head, and as he did so, Glen noticed a slight wobble in his stance.

"Here's the deal," he continued. "I might have been a tad delirious when Rosalie first arrived. I picked up some nasty tropical bug in the Philippines last month. I thought I had shaken it, but it came back with a vengeance last night. High fever, sweats, shakes, the whole nine. And don't ask about that smell, you don't want to know, trust me." Alan laughed again but it sounded thin, maybe even false. "But no worries, I put a call in to Dr. Chen. He had one of his boys from the all-night pharmacy bring me something, and I'm doing much better now. Really."

"Geez, Alan," Glen said, reaching out to feel Alan's forehead. "Tell me you will go in to see Dr. Chen today."

Alan swatted his hand away, laughing. "Christ, you two. You make me feel like I've got two moms. Of course I'm going in to see the doc. Look. You're taking the day off, remember? I'm taking the day off. And hell, even Rosalie's taking the day off. I called over to the cleaning service and told them to give her a paid day on my account. I love you guys, but you've got to stop the doting. You hear me?"

"Alright, boss." Glen pressed his lips together, then smiled. "I just don't know what we'd do if something happened to you."

Alan scoffed and rolled his eyes. "Get out of here, Glen, now you're being a sap. Oh, but two things before you go. First, there's a nice case of cabernet in the trunk of my car, the good stuff from France. Grab a bottle for your sister and one for Rosalie. Tell Rosalie I'm sorry for scaring her and tell your sister I'm sorry for not setting you up with a good woman yet."

"You're wasting your wine on Sophia. She's never going to like you no matter what you do, but I'm sure Rosalie will appreciate the gesture. What's the second thing?"

"Call the mayor and tell him I won't be able to attend tonight's gala. Offer him some dates next month."

"He'll be furious," Glen said, eyebrows raised.

"Of course he will, but I can't very well show up in my condition. If you and Rosalie can see through me, those guys will eat me alive. Besides, he's getting a bit big for his britches, needs to be knocked down a notch or two so he doesn't forget who is using who," Alan said. He was grinning broadly again, his eyes merry and shrewd. "I am the only reason he is where he is. He needs to remember that."

"Whatever secrets you two share, I don't want any part of it," Glen smirked. "But I will let him know you won't be there tonight. And I'll get a new event scheduled for the first week of November, right?"

"Good man," Alan clapped his shoulders. "Good man. Take it easy today, though, get that schedule straightened out then get your butt home. Do whatever it was you were doing before poor Rosalie got you all riled up. And don't forget the wine."

CHAPTER 9

GLEN HEADED SOUTH TOWARD SOPHIA'S house. He had taken both bottles of cab, but he knew Sophia would refuse the gift. "He's your friend," she'd say, "you drink it. If he gave a fuck about me, he wouldn't have stolen my brother away. If he really cared about you he would have cut you loose years ago, to live your own life. He's got you so wound around his finger, feeding your foolish obsession. The least he can do is give *you* the hoity-toity wine instead of trying to bribe me with it."

He thought about finishing her garden. He thought about Alan promising to make time for him after the gala, to talk about Glen getting on with his life, maybe turning the Constance Salvatore Project over to a new director. There were plenty of qualified candidates. He thought about the fact that Alan had promised this conversation several times over the last few months and as yet it hadn't happened.

It was a crisp autumn morning, the sun was bright. Glen wondered if it was bright enough to summon a mirage in the distance, if he looked at just the right angle, if he stared long enough. His heart sped up at the thought. He wondered if the flowers he placed at her shrine had wilted. They probably had. There was plenty of time left to till the garden, plenty of time left to plant before spring. When he reached Holman Avenue, he turned left instead of continuing straight to Sophia's house.

The corner grocer sold him a spray of white daisies and a small stuffed bear. They fit nicely with the other offerings at Connie's shrine. He sat on the log, watching intently for her ghost, but when the sun set that evening, she still had not appeared.

CHAPTER 10

OCTOBER SLIPPED INTO NOVEMBER, as it tends to do. Rosalie had accepted the wine apprehensively. She refused to discuss what happened with Alan that morning. "I think we should not talk about that. He say he was sick and now he better," she told him when he pressed her. "If you really need to know, maybe you talk to Dr. Chen."

"Doctors are not allowed to discuss their patients," Glen said.

"No? Well maybe he can say how he do an exam on Alan in his office here on the same day he do a conference in Dallas," Rosalie said, cocking one eyebrow.

"You're saying Alan never went to see Dr. Chen?" Glen asked.

"Did I say that? No. I say nothing. I can't talk about this, I've got babies to feed. Alan is a good man. He takes care of me. Maybe you take care of him, hmm?"

"I'll do what I can," Glen assured her, and let the matter rest.

He didn't mention why he was interested in Dr. Chen's schedule, but after a quick chat with the doctor's staff, he confirmed that the doctor was, in fact, in Texas the entire week in question. Maybe Alan had called a different doctor, but Glen was beginning to doubt that.

He didn't see Alan again until the night of the rescheduled gala. In the intervening weeks, Glen carried out his duties as project coordinator with waning enthusiasm. The shooting range, where he had taught Firearms for Personal Defense over the past four years, was going out of business. Glen considered asking Alan to just buy the place, but he figured that would be one more marker Alan would use to anchor him to The Project if he tried to leave. And he did intend to leave, didn't he? As the days passed and he spent more time away from Alan, Glen felt the man's hold on him slipping.

With Alan's funding and charisma, The Project had accomplished far more than Glen had ever dared dream. They had established four After School Safe Zones in some of the roughest inner city neighborhoods. Glen had a team of presenters who put on crime prevention skits and programs through all grades at the elementary and middle schools – antidrug, stranger danger, bully free, recognizing and reporting abuse.

Shortly after Alan joined Glen's little project, he donated a three story downtown office building to be used as The Project's headquarters. It's ground floor was a gym/dojo combination which served as the venue for The Project's several martial arts and self defense classes. First aid and CPR classes, gang awareness and prevention, community policing and various other programs were held in the classrooms and conference rooms on the second floor. The third floor held the administrative offices and a crisis intervention call center, as well as a secret suite of rooms reserved for CPS or the police as a temporary safe haven for abuse victims or witnesses.

Alan boldly proclaimed, to anyone and everyone who would listen, that The Project had singlehandedly cut violent crime in the city by over fifty percent. He claimed credit for the significant reduction in high school drug use and the resultant increase in graduation rates. He could tell you exactly how many people were walking around on those streets right now who would have been murdered if the city had been allowed to continue unchecked on its prior course.

In the early years, Alan had persuaded a young assistant district attorney to join their cause, then backed that man through his political career, pushing him all the way into the mayor's office. And soon that man, Mayor Anderson, would be a state senator. The Project had in fact reduced crime in the city so dramatically that the drop showed up on the state-wide crime stats.

By every measurable statistic, The Constance Salvatore Project was a success, a stunning success. Glen was coming to realize this was the very reason he no longer found solace there. He started The Project for two reasons and two reasons only – to find Connie's murderers, and to undo what had happened to her that night. It had succeeded fabulously in absolutely all that it attempted, except for those two things.

Logically, Glen knew nothing he did could ever bring Connie back, but a grieving mind has no use for logic. He had allowed himself to believe that somehow, if he rescued enough other people, it would make up for failing to rescue Connie. And if he could make up for that failure, maybe God or karma or the universe would...would what? Let her live again? Of course not, but...just maybe.

The logical analysis of his situation was that the Project had justified him remaining in the denial phase of his grief for almost nine years. That understanding had been insinuating itself into his mind for months now. It was an argument he could not win, but one he was not quite yet ready to concede.

As to finding her killers, The Project failed there as well. Three men had taken her, beat her, raped her. To conceal their crime, they left her to die under the wheels of a freight train. Only one was ever identified, Monty Goglioni, and that was by sheer coincidence. He had been killed in a shootout with police in an unrelated case. During a search of his car, the police discovered a stash of blood-stained girls underwear. One of these belonged to Connie.

The detectives had already stopped working her case by then. But having found a viable suspect, one who could offer no defense since he was dead, they called the case closed. Whoever the other two perpetrators had been, they got away free and clear, and nothing Glen or his whole Project accomplished managed to change that fact.

They hadn't brought Connie's killers to justice, and they hadn't undone what happened to her that night. Glen had to leave The Project. He could no longer accept the applause and the accolades for what he considered a failed endeavor.

CHAPTER 11

THE SECOND DAY OF NOVEMBER was drizzly and windy, not great weather for gardening, but that's exactly what Glen was doing. The shovel had been sticking out of the weedy garden patch for two weeks already and Sophia commented on it every time she saw him.

He had picked up a pair of rubber boots at the hardware store. Mud now coated the boots and his jeans up past his knees. He turned the dirt, one shovel-full at a time, burying dead weeds and exposing fresh black soil.

He saw Sophia through the sliding glass door between the back lawn and the dining room. She folded laundry, vacuumed, generally bustled about doing anything she could think of to pretend to ignore him. Twice, Glen caught her watching him through the glass. At first she had looked irritable, but as the morning wore on, her expression of annoyance turned to one of guarded optimism.

As he neared completion of the final row, the glass door rolled open. Sophia carried an umbrella in one hand and two large mugs in the other. Steam rose from the mugs, only to be whisked away by the restless autumn wind. She stepped gingerly through the wet grass.

"Jeeeesus, Glen," she called across the lawn. "What're ya doing out here, huh? Don't you know it's raining?"

"Hey, sis," Glen said. "I'm just tilling the garden, getting it ready to plant."

"Let me guess," she said, reaching him. "Alan sent you home with some magic beans?" She handed him a mug of cocoa. Her umbrella kept the rain off her head and face, but wind played havoc with her hair. She had long ago become an expert at hanging her bangs just right to cover the worst of her scar. Now, however, the gusts flipped her bangs this way and that, exposing the jagged rift that ran from her temple to the middle of her forehead.

"Nope, no beans, sis." Glen sipped at the cocoa, smiled, then took a deep swallow. "You put Kahlua in this," he said.

She nodded and smiled.

"You put a *lot* of Kahlua in this," he said taking another sip.

"Days like these, you gotta get warm any way you can."

Glen noted her red nose and rosy cheeks. "You look like you're staying plenty warm."

She flipped him a half-hearted bird with the hand holding her umbrella and sneered, but it was a mostly friendly sneer. He nodded at a shapeless heap by the corner of the raised bed. "Look under the tarp."

Sophia lifted the fluttering flap with the toe of her boot. What she saw startled a genuine smile out of her. As soon as she realized what had happened on her face, she twisted the smile into her typical wry grin. "Dahlia bulbs," she said.

"What, you don't like dahlias anymore?"

"Of course, I like dahlias. They've always been my favorite. But aren't you supposed to do that in the spring?"

"Well, that would be better, but this will be okay, I think. I might not be here in the spring." He didn't meet her eyes as he said this last, and hurried on before she could comment. "I picked up some weed cloth, too. I figure if I plant these now and throw the cloth down, you'll have something pretty to look at in your back yard this summer, and you shouldn't need to do much to maintain it."

She seemed to sober a bit, a tentative optimism sparkled just behind her eyes. "What's going on with you?"

Glen looked down at the dark mud and tangled roots. It wasn't something pretty to look at, not at all, but the potential was there. "No promises, Soph. Maybe there's something going on with me. I think maybe there is." He jabbed the spade at the scraggly weeds. "Can we talk about it when I come inside?"

"Yeah, Glen, I'd like that..." her smile faltered, "but I have to get ready for work. My shift starts in an hour."

Glen flicked his eyes at her spiked cocoa, "You're headed to work? As *warm* as you are?"

Sophia laughed through her teeth. "I work at a hospital laundry. My job is scraping blood and human waste off of white sheets. The *only* right way to do that job is drunk." She giggled a little. "Just ask my boss."

Glen raised his eyebrows. "As long as you aren't driving yourself. I'll give you a lift..."

"Oh, gawd! Glen! Give it a rest, would ya," she said, still laughing. "I'm not a victim for your damn project to rescue. Besides, I'm riding in with Dale."

"Lucky Dale."

"Oh, shut up, you." Her mug was empty, so she used the middle finger on that hand this time. "Listen," she said, serious now, "I'm off tomorrow night, but Dale has a fantasy football thing or some bullshit. Can we talk then?"

"Yeah, Soph, we can talk then."

She nodded and started for the house. "There's soup on the stove for you," she called back over her shoulder. "It's out of a can, but I made biscuits from scratch. They're in the oven...and don't you dare ask me *what* I scratched, 'cause I'm liable to tell you."

Glen chuckled. "I wouldn't dream of it."

"Of course not," she said. "You make sure you eat some. I'll know if you don't."

"I'll eat," Glen said. "I've been eating, can't you tell?"

She squinted at him, half way to the house by now. The blowing rain had soaked her lower half. Her bangs flapped up again, flashing the rift in her forehead. They watched each other across the wet grass for several seconds, each wondering whether the other would say something terrible like *I love you*. Eventually, Sophia voiced the sentiment in a slightly different phrase, "You take those wet clothes off before you come in. I don't want you tracking mud all over my house."

CHAPTER 12

"I'M GETTING OUT, SOPH," Glen told her over dinner the following evening. "I'm done."

"Really? What does Alan have to say about that?" she asked, not bothering to look up. "You haven't told him yet, have you?"

Glen shook his head. He had made spaghetti and they were eating it in the dining room instead of in front of the television.

"I have called over there twice. Rosalie says he's busy, says he can't talk right now."

"That's weird," Sophia said. "He's always got time for his favorite minion."

"Yeah, something's up with him. That's, I guess, part of the reason I made my decision. I saw something, a couple weeks back. I saw Alan with his mask off, just for the briefest of seconds, but it was there, for sure. He's a good man. He's like a father to me, my best friend, and has been for five years. But when I was there the other morning, he was someone else. He was scared. Alan's never scared of anything..."

Glen poked at an olive in his spaghetti, then continued. "Anyway, the point is, I think maybe I need to get away from here for a while, away from Alan, away from Connie, from this town. I have given Alan such a big part in my life, but he is someone other than who he pretends to be. I'm not saying he's intentionally hiding his true self, more like he's hiding *from* his true self. I think that's what I have been doing, too. I think maybe I'm someone other than I pretend to be, different than who I believe myself to be."

"Did you put oregano in this?" Sophia asked around a mouthful of spaghetti.

"Soph, this is important. You're not even listening."

"Yes I am," she said. She had been twirling pasta on her plate. Now, she raised her head and looked him straight in the eye. "You said you are having a midlife crisis and that I was right about Alan. Tell me something I don't already know."

"I also told you I'm done with The Project."

"And you said you haven't told Alan yet. Which means you are going to go in there to tell him. He's going to come up with some new program that only you can handle. He'll stroke your ego and poke your stupid self-absorbed guilt, and you'll feel like you have no choice but to stay on — 'at least through the winter.' I can't remember shit, but I do remember having this conversation with you at least twice already."

Glen smiled. He slid a folder across the table to her. "Take a look."

Sophia did not look at the folder, not at first. She pinned Glen with a look he remembered from childhood. Then it had been their mother staring at him with a slight wrinkle between her eyebrows, half worry, half you-better-not-be-jerking-my-chain anger. "Is this just more bullshit, Glen? I'm too old and worn-out for anymore bullshit."

"Just open it, Soph."

Her eyes fell to the folder. She stuffed a bite of spaghetti into her mouth, then opened it. The top sheet was a letter of resignation. Its first line read, *Dear Alan, I quit.* Sophia chortled. "Straight to the point. You should have just left it there. The rest of this letter is kissing his ass and telling him how great a guy he really is?"

"Of course," Glen grinned. "But that first line is all that matters, right? I, uh, I already mailed it, too. This is just the copy I kept for my records. Look at the next page."

The next page was enrollment papers at a community college in the town of Oakville, three hours away.

"Oakville?" Sophia asked, mischief twinkled in her eyes. "Isn't that where Rochelle lives now?"

"Huh, I guess it is," Glen said, "imagine that."

"I told you, no more bullshit," Sophia said, smiling. "She called me a while back. I told you that, right?"

"Oh, now who's full of bullshit? You didn't tell me that and you know it."

"Huh, must have forgot...So, yeah, Rochelle called, wanted to know if you were for real this time or if you were still caught in your stupid time warp."

"So you already knew about all this?" Glen asked, gesturing to the folder.

"I don't know nothing, Glen, not 'till I see it with my own eyes," she said, "and that's what I told Rochelle. If you're really for real about making a clean break from Alan and Connie and all that tragedy, then thank god, it's about fucking time. I'm all for it. I'll support you any way I can. But if you're just fucking around again, breaking hearts and wasting everybody's time, I don't want to hear about it."

"Is that what you told Rochelle?"

"I told that girl that when you are present in the here and now, you're the best man I know. But then I told her she shouldn't be playing second fiddle to any woman, and certainly not to some dead girl..."

"Would you stop calling her that..."

"No! I will not! Connie was sweet and cute and

wonderful. But now she's dead. She died. You didn't. Until you get that through your head...god damn it, Glen! Where's the fucking wine? You can't serve spaghetti without wine."

Glen drew a deep breath. *Can't serve* you *anything without wine*, he thought, then instantly hated himself for it. She had been so sweet before the accident, so kind. Glen believed that had been the true Sophia. She hadn't been the same since waking from her coma. Perhaps the damage to her brain physically altered her personality. The doctors had warned them of that possibility. Or perhaps this cruder, meaner façade was just her defense against the particular cruelties of her life. Either way, who was he to begrudge her a drink or five?

He grabbed a bottle from the pantry – the cabernet Alan had given him, not that he would tell Sophia this – and returned to the table. The cork made a hollow pop as he pulled it. "Hey, Soph, can we hit rewind? Let's edit out that last exchange, right. Go back to what you told Rochelle?"

"You tell me Connie's dead and you accept that fact, and I'll tell you what I told Rochelle."

Glen poured two glasses and set one in front of her. "Connie's dead. I accept that."

"And being Alan's most prized gopher isn't going to fix it."

"Agreed," Glen said.

Sophia eyed him warily, then spoke, "I told Rochelle she should give you a chance, just a little chance, and not to get her hopes up. I told her if you fuck up again I'm going to beat you bloody. And I'm telling you now, Rochelle is a sweet girl who used to love you and maybe can again if you manage to keep your head out of your own asshole. She deserves to be somebody's one-and-only. And I think she wants that somebody to be you. But if you break her heart again, I swear on the pope and all his cronies, I'm going to fucking bury you under the fucking dahlias. Fair enough?"

"That's what you told her?"

"Something like that," Sophia said. She took a long swallow of the wine, then refilled her glass.

Glen nodded. "I can live with that," he said, then smiled. "Actually, both times *I* called her, she hung up on me. You probably weren't supposed to tell me she called you."

Sophia burst out in a short laugh. "Oops," she said. "Now that you mention it, I guess maybe she did ask me not to say anything...but you know how my memory gets these days."

Glen chuckled.

"Big sister's got your back again, huh?" she said raising her glass.

Glen clinked her glass with his own. "You do come in handy from time to time."

"Aw, you're so sweet," she said. "No wonder that poor girl is panting for you."

"Okay, Soph, that's enough of that," Glen said. "I've got a favor to ask, it's serious. You're probably not going to like it, but it's important."

"Oh, God, now what?"

"I need to say good-bye...to Alan," he paused, "and to Connie. One last time. I will see Alan at the gala. Either he will talk to me or I'll announce my resignation on my own. But Connie, I, um...I'd like you to go with me. You know, so I don't get lost while I'm there, so I can remember what I'm there for..."

"So you don't gork out and stare into space until you die of hypothermia?"

"Yeah, something like that. Maybe let me talk a bit about her. You never wanted to hear it before, and I understand why, but I just want to say a few words and I want someone to hear the words. I need to make my peace with the place."

Sophia pursed her lips, considering. Finally she said, "Yeah, I'll take you out there. I'll listen to your speech or whatever. Just so long as you promise it really is the last time – I won't ever have to send someone out to that damn railroad crossing to look for you again."

Glen promised.

CHAPTER 13

CONNIE'S SHRINE HAD ORIGINALLY BEEN just a wide tree trunk which Glen, Connie's parents, and a few friends had festooned with flowers and hand drawn cards. Over the week following her death, pinwheels and tinsel and teddy bears had accumulated. All that was long gone now. The acute pain of tragedy, however horrible, can't compete long with the day-in-day-out distractions, pains, necessities of ongoing life. Connie died in May, by the end of July the shrine was nothing more than a tattered, faded blur by the side of the road.

For a couple of years the shrine's only visitor was Glen, and Connie's parents sometimes. Then, after their feeble citizen's against crime initiative grew wings and became the Constance Salvatore Project – after Alan joined and put his financial muscle behind it, that is – the city council installed a plaque and a small covered booth just to the side of the road.

The plaque told a Disneyfied version of Connie's murder. It then extolled the accomplishments of the Project launched in her name. Next came an admonition to report suspicious activity. It concluded with a reminder to keep children away from train tracks. Whenever Glen left his flowers, he did his best to arrange them so they covered that stupid plaque.

Now, he walked past the shrine without looking at it. The sun had set, but the sky still glowed in its fading light. It had been warm for a November day, but the temperature was dropping, and as it did, thick fog rose out of the damp ground.

"Where you going, Glen? This is your log right here," Sophia called, stopping only a stone's throw from the road.

Glen stopped, standing between the rails, and lowered his head. "That's not where she died, Soph," he said. He didn't turn back to her, just seemed to huddle into himself a bit, then added, "I see her, sometimes, a little further down the track."

"And you expect me to go walking down there in the dark?" she said. "I thought we were just going to the crossing. I'm not going under the viaduct, no fucking way, buddy."

Glen stiffened. "It's just this side of the viaduct, up on top of the tracks. We won't be going under...This is the last time, I promise."

Sophia crunched along the granite chunks of railway underlayment, then walked between the rails until she reached him. "This is the last time. *That* is something I will not forget. You understand me?"

Glen nodded and took her hand. She flinched just a bit, and her eyes widened, but she did not comment.

As they moved away from the crossing, the ground on either side of the tracks fell away at a steep incline. A thin forest blocked the view to their right, its trunks and shrubs already veiled by darkness. To their left, the roofs of a housing development stretched off into the misty dusk. The houses replaced a ratty trailer park that had stood there the night Connie died.

The woods had been here since before Glen's childhood. He and Connie had explored every inch of them. A thin stream wound its way through the forest then shot straight as an arrow down a concrete lined gully on the residential side of the tracks. A single stone archway, the viaduct, opened like the mouth of a cavern under the rail line, connecting these two disparate sides of the same creek. It also allowed for a foot path connecting the trailer court to the forest and the homes that lay beyond it.

When the stone retention wall surrounding the viaduct appeared out of the gathering fog, Glen stopped. "This is the place," he whispered.

The woods seemed to advance closer to the tracks

as the gloom there deepened. Holman Avenue, where Sophia had parked, lay fifty yards behind them. About twice that distance ahead of them, they could see the lights of traffic crossing Stave Avenue. Street lamps and back porch lights popped on in the neighborhood to their left. A high chain link fence blocked access between the houses and the tracks. Three strands of barbed wire ran along its top. But even from here, Glen could see a hole had been cut through the fence at the mouth of the viaduct. Places like this seemed to have a drawing power, a power that called to children and predators alike.

"God," Sophia muttered. Glen felt her shudder. "This is an evil place. We knew that back when I was a girl. You knew it too. Mom and dad must have told you a hundred times to stay out of there. I know I sure as hell told you. Why would she have come out here after dark?"

"It wasn't dark yet," Glen said. "She was here because...she was here because I was going to be here. She knew I was coming to her house. I took the shortcut through the woods to beat curfew. She knew I was coming, so she came out to meet me."

"But you tripped over a root and cracked your head on a tree and she met up with that Goglioni character instead," Sophia said, her voice low but angry. "And not one single piece of that story makes you even a little bit responsible for what happened."

"We always knew what the other was thinking..."

"Bullshit!" Sophia hissed. "You're going to tell me you should have known she was in trouble? That you should have somehow Twilight Zoned it? And what if you had? Huh? What would you have done, called that Officer Tubbaguts who used to sleep in his patrol car out here?"

"Soph..."

"Or what?" she persisted, "You were gonna run out here and fight those guys yourself? That's stupid."

"Sophia! Please, just...just stop, okay? Or go back to the car? Let me do what I got to do and I'll be there in just a few minutes."

"Hell, no. I'm not going back to the fucking car! I told you this is an evil place. I'm not walking around out here by myself and I sure as hell ain't leaving my little brother out here in the dark by himself," she said. "So say what you gotta say and lets get out of here."

"Fine. But no more talking. Period."

"Fine," she scoffed.

"Wait here," he said, letting go of her hand. He walked a few paces further. Sophia stayed right behind him, pace for pace. Glen looked back at her, annoyed, but said nothing.

He knelt down when he reached the spot. Not a single shred of evidence remained from that night eight years ago. Nearly every drop of Connie's blood had been spilled here – staining these ties, draining through the granite stones beneath them – but what the crime lab left, the elements had long since erased. Sometime the year following her death, Glen came to this spot and carved her name into the tie, to ensure he could always find it, but he had never needed that marker.

Glen reached into his shirt and pulled out the silver cross he wore around his neck. It had been Connie's, though she only wore it for special occasions. Her parents had given it to Glen after her death. He placed the cross on a tie that had once been painted in her blood, then sat motionless for several minutes. Crickets sang in the woods to his right. Somewhere to his left a bass line thumped dully. All around them, fog rose like an incoming tide.

"I'm sorry, Connie," Glen finally said, his voice choked with tears. "I'm so sorry. If there was any way...anything I could do to change what happened..." He stifled a sob. "If I could just have one chance to take it back, to do it over...I'd give my life for a second chance, Connie..." He sniffed and shook and started again, "That's all I've been praying for, all these years...but it doesn't work that way, I guess. You only get one shot, one chance to do it right, but if you fu...if you mess it all up, it stays messed up for good."

"There's lots of people, probably hundreds of

people who are alive today because of things we did in your name. I know that's not much comfort to you. It wasn't any comfort to you while you...while you were dying...But that's the best I can do. That's the only thing I can do...I hope it's enough. Wherever you are, I hope what we did in your name brings you some joy or comfort or at least some peace.

"But Connie, I have to move on now. I have to accept that I failed. I failed to save you, I failed to find the...the others, who were here...but I have to stop failing. I have to...to go forward. I won't be coming here anymore. This is not a good place. Not for me. Not for you. I won't be coming here anymore and I hope you won't be coming here either. I thought I kept coming back here for you, but I wonder. Maybe this whole time you were coming back for me. I'm sorry I wasn't here for you when you needed me. I'm sorry I've kept you here so long. Please move on, Connie. Go wherever it is angels are supposed to go when they're done here. Please don't come here any more and I promise I won't come here again, either. Please forgive me. I love you...that's all."

His words hung in the mist and darkness. Sophia's hand closed over his shoulder, warm and solid. Glen waited, feeling there was some final piece of this farewell yet to complete. One-hundred yards past the viaduct, where Stave Avenue crossed the tracks, a slow-moving bus trundled over the rails. As it did so, the fog glowed with the florescent light from its windows. The bus's glow backlit a figure, a silhouette in the middle of the tracks. It stood, arms at its side, just above the viaduct. In the fog and darkness, it could have been anybody, but Glen knew it was Connie. Just as the bus passed and the lighted fog faded, she bent one arm at the elbow, waving good-bye.

Glen's breath caught in his throat. His heart gave a single kick, then seemed to stop completely. Half of him wanted to race forward before her image faded, wanted to wrap his arms around her and never let her go. The other half was too terrified to move.

Her voice in his head sounded the way it always had when they were young, the way it always did in his dreams. It came through in a whispered rush that easily could have been mistaken for the wind, had there been any. Two statements, overlapping, "I forgive you. I did long ago," in his left ear, "maybe someday you will, too," in his right.

He nearly screamed when a second hand closed on his shoulder. "We need to go now," Sophia said in a hushed voice.

"You heard it, too?"

"I didn't hear shit," Sophia said, so resolutely it had to be a lie, "except for you promising ghost girl you wouldn't ever come back here. I'm leaving and if you don't come now, you're walking home."

He didn't have time to think about it. Sophia hooked her arm under his and dragged him backward. He staggered to his feet, turned, and walked with her as if in a dream. To the left, forest critters chittered and squeaked. On the other side, couples argued and babies squalled. Behind them, more busses crossed the tracks at Stave, but no silhouette darkened the thickening mist.

CHAPTER 14

CONNIE'S PICTURE HUNG ABOVE THE stage, the same picture that had adorned her shrine, only this one was nearly fifteen feet tall. Above her face, large letters proclaimed "The Constance Salvatore Project." A tag along the bottom read, "Saving lives. Changing the world. It's in your hands."

Glen hated it.

It no longer reminded him of Connie, not even a little bit. That picture had become an empty icon, a symbol inviting donors to fill it with whatever meaning motivated them to 'change the world'. This was an effective ploy, giving The Project a more universal appeal, drawing support from all sectors. But Glen wasn't here for all sectors, he was here for Connie.

The giant floating head with its feel-good slogans and mass appeal reinforced Glen's conviction it was time to walk away. Connie had become all sorts of things to these people, but she had ceased to be the girl

Glen had grown up with, the girl he had fallen in love with.

He sat at the head table, watching Alan work his magic on this wealthy crowd of would-be do-gooders, and decided they could keep the Connie Alan had invented for them. And he would keep his Connie. She had been adventure and mystery and a depth of wonder these people would never understand. Glen never understood it either, really, but he had known it was there, had expected to spend a lifetime discovering her mysteries, as she discovered his.

Applause rumbled through the banquet hall. Alan had just delivered one of his soul stirring lines, probably the one about the power of a united people standing arm and arm against the evil in our midst. Glen, himself, had loved that line – the first fifty times he heard it. He couldn't resent these people, the benefactors of the project he had created. He couldn't resent Alan for infusing his project with the capital and charisma Glen never could have hoped to provide. But the whole thing felt hollow, like a body without a soul. Glen guessed it had felt this way for quite some time, but he was only now allowing himself to acknowledge it.

Sophia had offered to accompany him to the gala – whether to provide moral support by her presence, or to spur his courage by kicking his shins under the table,

Glen didn't know – but he had declined her offer. As he sat next to Alan's empty seat, listening to the crowd laugh at one of Alan's anecdotes, he had no doubt in his ability to go through with his resignation. A confirmation of his class schedule from Oakville Community College had arrived in that morning's mail. Rochelle had picked up the phone today for the first time in recent memory. Their conversation had been short and awkward. She had been about to go into an appointment when he called. He suspected the only reason she picked up this time was that she had an easy excuse to terminate the call quickly. But still, she *had* picked up. And she had stated she was glad he was moving to Oakville. It wasn't much, but it was a start, a glimmer.

Alan's words washed over him like surf polishing stones on a rocky shoreline. He had heard it all before. The rhetoric had done its work on him until there was no work left to do. To the audience, however, it was new, exhilarating. They responded as predictably as rubes at an old time carnival. And Alan was in fine form. He had them eating out of his hand, hanging on every word. Glen mused that whatever malaise had afflicted Alan over the past weeks, he was now recovered completely.

As Alan's talk neared its conclusion, Glen's pulse quickened. He was supposed to speak next, as he always had, detailing the specifics of each of The Project's programs. Glen was a fine public speaker, certainly not a ring master like Alan, but more than competent. It wasn't the speaking that had raised his heart rate, it was the *not* speaking. Alan had to have received Glen's resignation, either yesterday or this morning, Glen didn't know, nor did it matter. What did matter was that Alan had not said or done anything to acknowledge it, so Glen would have to force the issue.

"And now," Alan announced, "I am honored to introduce to you the man who's vision and passion brought this project into existence, a man who's tireless dedication and unfaltering sense of purpose has built our little organization into one of the most successful citizen action groups in the entire country. Glen McClay, ladies and gentlemen."

The whole room rose to their feet clapping as enthusiastically as decorum allowed. Glen also rose, bowing slightly, then joined Alan on the stage. Alan spoke again as the applause died down, reminding them all that Glen had grown up with Connie, had known her better than anyone here besides her parents. That her loss had effected him so deeply he had decided to do something about it. He spoke of Glen's courage and persistence, and finally concluded the introduction with, "Glen has some thrilling stories to share with you about what you have accomplished this year and some exciting news about new proposals for the months to come. So, please, one more round of applause for Glen McClay!"

More applause. As the donors quieted, Glen made his thank-yous and welcomes. The microphone felt too heavy. His knuckles gripped it so tightly they turned white. *Here we go,* he thought, and launched into the shortest speech of his career.

"As Alan promised I have exciting news. I can't hold your attention the way he does, so I'll get right to it. I have been the Programs Director since the Project began, but tonight I would like to present Mary Beth Cruchfield, who I have appointed Interim Programs Director. I will be stepping aside for a while. Mary Beth has been with us almost since the beginning. She knows more about the programs than I do. After a few months with her at the helm, you are all going to wonder what you needed me for in the first place. So, with out any further ado, Mary Beth Cruchfield!"

He handed her the mic and stepped to the side. The crowd hesitated just a beat, then erupted in yet another round of applause. Glen made his way off the stage, back to his seat at the head table. He noticed Alan staring blankly ahead, no expression at all on his face, as if he was trying to decide who to be in the next moment.

By the time Glen reached his chair, Alan had

decided. "I bet you thought that was going to be a surprise," Alan whispered, now wearing a sly grin. "I hope it wasn't a surprise for her."

"Of course not," Glen said, his pulse thudding rapidly at his temples. "I made sure she was ready. I'm stepping down, Alan, but I still care what happens here."

Mary Beth faltered a bit on her opening sentences. The crowd received her with warm interest. When her gaze travelled to the head table, Alan smiled at her. Glen knew the power of that smile and felt a moment of jealousy. The effect on Mary Beth was comically amazing, though Glen supposed only he and Alan noticed. Her eyes lit, her shoulders straightened, any hint of hesitation left her voice. She found her rhythm then, and delivered the remainder of her address with the smooth confidence of the professional she was.

Mary Beth's speech was followed by a twenty-five minute professionally produced video praising the virtues of the Constance Salvatore Project, clips of program participants learning martial arts at the dojo or firearms safety at the range, bits of news footage about the difference the Project had made in one community or another, happy kindergarteners singing safety songs, footage of Glen demonstrating CPR on a dummy. It was beautiful, but Connie wasn't mentioned once.

The remainder of the night passed exactly as every

other function had. They ate their dinners, sipped their champagne. Alan pretended nothing had changed. Glen suspected Alan actually believed nothing had. Socializing and public relations had opposite effects on the two men, to Glen it was a burden, but It energized Alan. They would have their talk, as Alan had promise, but not until Glen was thoroughly worn out.

As the crowd thinned, Alan leaned close to Glen and said, "Let's move to the back of the room," he nodded toward an empty table in the dimly lit corner. "We'll have more privacy there."

Glen twisted a wry smile and thought, for the second time that night, *here we go*. He followed Alan around the outside edge of the room, the two of them disappearing into the carefully orchestrated shadows, to the table he had suggested. Only two chairs waited, rather than eight as had been afforded each of the other tables. This table was also the farthest one from an exit, and although the table itself was very private, no exit could be reached from it without walking through a crowd or directly under the glow of spotlights.

"You really set this up well," Glen said, expecting a bit of banter before they got into the meat and bones of their talk.

Alan wasn't interested in banter. "Do you really think you can just walk away? Just like that?"

"Please, don't try to stop me."

75

"Oh, that's not what I mean. You have been so hung up on this girl for eight years. She has consumed your life. How are you just going to walk away now?"

"But that's just the point. The Constance Salvatore Project hasn't been about Connie for years now. That's not the girl I knew," Glen waved an arm at the giant floating head hovering above the stage. "The girl I knew is gone – gone long ago. It's time I be gone, too.

"This Project is all you now, anyway," Glen continued. "I haven't been relevant here in years. I make a good poster boy. I have an interesting connection to Connie. But everything you do here you can keep right on doing without me..."

"Glen. Stop right there. I have never known a more loyal or dedicated person. You created this. You are responsible for everything we have accomplished here. Sure it has grown beyond your initial vision, but look. Look!" Alan made a broad sweeping motion with his arm. He looked like one of the legendary emperors of old, Ozymandias perhaps, presenting the glories of his kingdom to a travelling stranger. "All of these people are here because *you* had the heart and the vision to bring them together."

"I'm done," Glen said, as flatly as he could manage without raising his voice.

Alan pulled an irritated grimace, making a *calm down* motion with his hands. "I know, I know, Glen. I got your letter, and then you go and pull this little stunt," he nodded toward the table where Mary Beth was being overwhelmed by well-wishers and reporters. "That was a clever checkmate, by the way," Alan's sly smile revealed a hint of admiration. "I'm glad you made sure she had a speech prepared, but it might have been nice of you to prepare her for the aftermath." Mary Beth's plate of chicken cordon bleu had barely been touched, and the wait staff hadn't even bother to bring her dessert.

Glen grinned, "She'll get used to it. The attention will do her good. You take good care of her, Alan."

Alan pretended offence. "I always took care of you, didn't I?"

Glen nodded.

"I took care of you too well, seems to me," Alan said. "How much money do you have squirreled away, huh? Enough to live on while you finish your degree? Enough to take care of Sophia if she takes a turn?"

"You have paid me well, Alan," Glen said. "You financed my dream, and you did so in grand style. I couldn't have asked for a better boss – "

"Boss?" Alan sounded genuinely offended this time. "We are partners, Glen! We have been from the very beginning. And we still are, regardless of this...whatever it is you are going through. Do you remember that morning you came stumbling into my

77

office with your hand-drawn pamphlets and your 'dream of a better community?' You were what, fifteen years old?"

Glen's lips bent up in a grim, determined smile. "You're not going to make this easy, are you?"

"Why would I?" Alan asked. His tone was still friendly, but exasperation simmered just below the surface. "You and I, Glen. You've been like the little brother I never had. I don't understand why you would want to walk away from all this, from what we've built together."

"Alan, I have infinite respect for you. Without your guidance, the Project would have died before it even got off the ground. And I, I don't know how I would have survived those first few years after her death. I can never thank you enough..."

"But?" Alan asked.

"But I can't do this anymore. I have been lying to myself all these years. Back when I was a grieving teenager, I guess that was okay, but I'm an adult now. I always told myself that what we were doing here was about Connie, for Connie. I was still trying to save her, believing somehow I *could* save her," Glen spread his hands, "but I can't, can I?"

Alan stared at him, eyes burning in the dim light, burning darker somehow.

"This has never been about Connie," Glen

continued. "She died, and nothing I do can ever change that. This Project was about me, about me trying to hide from a mistake I made, trying to cover up or fix that mistake...and I can't. I think I have finally come to terms with that fact, or at least I am ready to start coming to terms with it."

"What mistake? Tell me that, Glen. That's the thing we all want to know."

The change had come over Alan again, and it chilled Glen in a way he could barely comprehend. Something bright and dangerous danced behind the man's eyes. Glen saw fear there, as he had seen on the morning Rosalie called him. But more than fear, there was also a predatory gleam in Alan's eyes. Glen had seen this there from time to time, usually just before Alan strong-armed a politician or CEO into supporting The Project. But this was deeper, more fundamental to the man's being.

"What has gotten into you?" Glen asked. "Ever since that morning last month, when you rescheduled this gala, there's been something wrong with you. Are you still sick? Is that it?"

"Don't make this about me. I'm not the one who's walking away."

"Hey, take it easy. I'm just concerned about you."

"I'm not sick. I'm healthier than ever, might live to be a hundred and ten if things keep going as they are."

The fear was in Alan's voice now, but he covered it with indignant exasperation. Alan was maneuvering Glen into place to close some deal, trying to force Glen to accept some proposal he had not yet even laid out. "Now listen to me, Glen, I don't like to lose. You know that about me. And I certainly don't want to lose you. Especially to some ill-conceived whim or early on-set midlife crisis.

"Look, I need you," Alan continued, "You and I are connected, our lives interwoven, far more closely than you know. We are here for the exact same reasons, and if we are here together, it works, but if you go, as you seem intent on doing, I have no reason to stay."

"What are you talking about?" Glen asked.

"Something happened," Alan said. He looked down at the table for several minutes before looking back to Glen. "Something happened the other morning, before you came by the house..." He drew a long, shuddering breath and waved a hand at the waiters loitering at the back of the room. "If we start down this road, Glen, we have to go all the way. You keep saying it is your fault Connie died. You've never said that before these last few months. Tell me what happened that night, help me understand where this guilt is coming from."

"Why? What does that have to do with anything?"

"Demons, Glen. You are getting ready to run from

yours and I am here to tell you, it *will not* work. Wherever you go, however you try to get away – you can change your face, you can change your name, it doesn't matter – they will always find you. You can't run from your demons. If you face them now, while it is still your choice, there may yet be hope. But if you turn and run..." Alan shook his head, as if miserable and disappointed.

The waiter approached, beaming a solicitous smile. When he saw Alan's face, the smile vanished. Alan barked, "Bring us two Cokes and a bottle of bourbon." The waiter spun to the task without a word.

Glen sat transfixed, mesmerized. This Alan was someone he barely recognized. "You are scaring me. What is wrong with you?"

"I told you, something happened. I understand now, the world beneath the world," he said. "I'm trying to help you understand as well. You *need* to understand."

"What is it you want from me?"

"I want to know what happened that night. I want you to admit the truth. Not that it matters much to me, I never knew the girl, but it means everything to you, to get it out in the open. What really happened? You have been lying to everyone, most especially to yourself, ever since that night and I'm trying to tell you, that will not work. Sooner or later, your demons will come for you, as mine have for me, and when they do, the only way to face them is in stark naked honesty."

The waiter returned and placed two tumblers of Coke and the bourbon on the table. He was about to ask if they needed anything else, then he got another look at Alan's face and decided that loitering with is buddies might be a better idea.

The interruption gave Glen a moment to catch up. He had never seen Alan like this. Alan's Roman emperor face had always seemed incapable of displaying fear or any vulnerable emotion, but now desperation and perhaps even dread crept across it. There was also an unsettling degree of morbid resignation, like a man staring down an onrushing locomotive, simultaneously lusting for and fearing dark obliteration.

"I love you like a brother, Glen. I'm not trying to make you stay with the Project. It's too late for that. Too late for both of us now. I'm trying to make you understand – whether you stay or go, there is no way out. Your demons will find you, and when they do, you had better be ready to face them.

"That story about waking up in the woods and not remembering isn't going to cut it. When your past catches up, when your demons find you and demand their pound of flesh, you have to pay!" Alan sat back a little, eyes burning. He poured a slug of liquor into his Coke and took a long, slow sip. Glen didn't once take his eyes off this strangely darker man.

Alan started in again, a little calmer now. "I don't suspect we'll see each other again after tonight, not with what I'm about to say. I will tell you the truth about me, as much as I can bear. When I've finished you won't like me anymore. You won't feel so compelled to win my approval. Maybe then you can tell me what happened in the woods that night."

Glen interrupted, "I don't understand what this is about...."

Alan held up a hand. "You will understand, in just a few moments, you will understand more than you want to, I suspect. But I think you owe it to me to listen. Will you do at least that much before you go? Will you hear me out?"

Glen nodded. "As long as you understand, it doesn't matter what you say, I am no longer part of this Project."

Alan waved this away as if it were utterly inconsequential. "You are talking about the future, Glen, and that no longer matters. Not at all, as you will soon come to understand. What matters now, the only thing that matters, is the past – my past, and your past. I will tell you mine and you will tell me yours, and then I think we will be finished with each other, perhaps for good."

Glen sighed, perplexed. "Well, go ahead then, I

guess."

Alan smiled as if he had just won a hard fought victory. He drank off a third of his spiked Coke and refilled his glass from the bourbon bottle. Then his face hardened and he began to speak.

CHAPTER 15

"WHEN YOU MET ME, I was only two years into my life as a productive member of society. I had a new name, a new profession, I even had a new face. You know I grew up rough, but you don't realize the extent of it. I made my fortune in real estate investments and urban development, as you know, but the seed money for my first ventures – that all came from my former profession.

"When I was a kid, I lived with my mom, her sister, their cousin Jenny, and the seven other children that belonged to them. We lived in a trailer, in a trailer court, in a part of town where people who have money don't go.

"I vowed to myself that I was not going to end up being a loser like them, spending my days in some miserable crappy trailer. I was already taking money to stand lookout for the pushers, so it was an easy transition to become a dealer myself.

"Yeah, Glen, don't look so surprised. I was one of them. I am a survivor, a winner. I always have been. If there is a way to succeed, I will find it. Where I came up, the opportunities I had, I made the best of them. I worked the system I was born into, and I worked it better than anyone else. I stayed in school. My top lieutenants did as well. That's where all our customers hung out. By the time I graduated, I was well on my way to becoming an American drug lord. I mainly ran weed and meth, a lot of weed and meth, but I had connections – I could get you anything you needed.

"To succeed in that business you have to be smart enough not to get caught, and you have to be ruthless." Alan spread his hands, a bemused smile twitched the corners of his lips. "You know me, I was both."

"By the time I was twenty, I ran my own cartel. I had supply lines, safe houses. I had a handful of bright young students in the elementary and Jr. high developing new clientele for my operation. I even had a semi-legit accountant running my money for me. Not only that, we were quiet. We conducted most of our business on the deep down low. The cops knew drugs were pouring into the community, but they had no idea where it was coming from. They never had a clue who I was. Carl Withers – that's the name I was born with – has no criminal record, and never did."

The darkness in his demeanor subsided, just a little,

subverted by something else. Glen realized it was pride he heard in Alan's voice. He may not be proud of what he had done, but he was sure proud of how well he had done it. Even to this day.

"They only got close once, the cops, that is, and that was pure luck – good luck on their part, bad on ours." Alan's voice darkened again. He paused, seeming to gather his thoughts, or perhaps his courage. "I'll tell you about that in a minute, but first I need to tell you about Jerry. I think Jerry is where I really changed, where I finally became what I am today.

"He was the shop keeper across the street from one of my stash houses – a good guy, a likeable guy. He did this after-school tutoring thing in the basement of his shop, teaching kids the basic reading and math stuff they needed to get through a day at school. We all liked him. We'd say 'hi,' when we passed on the street.

"The problem was, he knew I was dealing. Jerry asked to meet with me, wanted to show me something at his shop. I said sure, why not. He took me down in the basement, told me about the work he was doing with the kids, explained how investing in the community provides more economic opportunities for future generations and all that.

"Then he confronted me about my business, said he wanted to have a man to man talk about my impact on the community. I don't know what this guy was thinking. I guess I come across as easy going and reasonable. Maybe I am today, but that sure as hell wasn't the case back then.

"He told me he wanted me to stop selling to the kids he tutored. He said he knew there would always be dealers, it was a problem that would never go away, but he wanted me to leave his students alone so they could grow to fulfill his vision for a better tomorrow.

"Well, I was offended, to say the least. But I'm a business man, right? So, I told this guy sure, I'll stop selling to your students. No problem. I'll just tally up how much money that will cost me and I'll send you a bill at the end of each month. As long as you pay, I'll stay away from your kids.

"He said there was no way in hell he was going to pay protection money to a small time thug like me. Things kinda when down hill from there. I never carried a gun back then. Guns are loud and imprecise, the opposite of my philosophy. But Jerry had a gun, a snub-nose .357 magnum. He said 'I gave you a chance and you blew it.' He pulled his gun with one hand and grabbed the phone with his other. 'I know you have a pile of dope next door, and I know a certain detective who would love to have a look at it.'

"He didn't make that call," Alan said. Glen watched him replaying the scene behind his eyes. He spoke matter-of-factly, now, just reporting the events, emotions stowed for later retrieval. "Never pull a gun unless you mean to use it. You know that as well as anyone. I charged him as he started dialing. He had a chance to shoot, plenty of time, really, but he hesitated. I took his gun away and put two bullets in his chest. We robbed the store, to make it look good, moved the stash house that night, and went right on with business as usual.

"But, something happened in my mind that night. I went from drug lord to minor god. I had never killed before, hadn't really even thought about killing, but that wasn't what changed me. The thing was, I had brought a knife to a gunfight, and I had won. After that, I always carried the piece with me.

"I never used it again, but it became a talisman, a symbol. It meant I was invincible. If I had been pinched, that gun would have connected me to Jerry's murder. But that didn't matter. The gun stayed in my jacket pocket from then on. Any time I got into a sticky situation, I felt it there," Alan patted the left side of his chest where the pistol would have hung, "and I knew I'd never get caught."

Alan's glass was half empty. He topped it up with bourbon. Glen stared at him, trying to disbelieve but finding it impossible. Alan's voice rang with the validity of his confession. Glen had so many questions but was unable to formulate any one of them.

"Yeah, Glen, it's bad," Alan said, "and it gets worse, a lot worse. I'm not sure I want to tell the rest of it."

"I'm not sure I want to hear it," Glen said, bewildered.

"No, you don't. That's one thing I am sure of, but you *need* to hear it. And once you do, you'll understand why." He drank his drink in three big swallows, then filled the empty glass with straight bourbon. It occurred to Glen then that he had never seen Alan drink before. He went ahead and had a swallow of his own Jack and Coke.

"I told you the cops nearly caught me one time," Alan started again. "There was a bit of disputed turf, nothing of much consequence, just a few rows of those sprawling trailer courts on the south side, but the outfit crowding our guys out of the courts looked like they meant to move in on our territory in a big way.

"We needed to set them back a bit, quell their ambitions. I grabbed a couple of my runners, armed them with pipes and spiked baseball bats, and we raided the rival dealer's stash house. We were quick and quiet – I had that .357, but never used it – we just went in with clubs and knifes, and it was almost perfect.

"The punks guarding the stash got the worst of it. I'll spare you the details, but all of them ended up in the hospital. Two of them died. Those who survived did their recovering in prison. But one of my kids, Twinkie we called that one, he caught a bullet with his liver. I sent the rest of my guys off on foot – someone called the cops when the gunfire started – and I dragged Twinkie into an Escalade the other gang owned. He was alive when I put him in the back seat, but died before we had gone two blocks.

"There must have been a patrol car already cruising the area, because he was on me before I even left the curb. As soon as that pig got behind us, he lit us up.

"We all knew how to ditch the cops on foot, but over the road was a different story. I hadn't planned on taking that Escalade, so I had no escape route in mind. If I knew Twinkie wasn't gonna make it, I would have just dumped it and ran, but it was too late for that.

"The surface streets back to my side of town were cut off by a train. My only other option was the freeway. That pig was tight on my tail. The escalade had a police scanner, and I could hear the other units responding. The train had slowed them down as well, but it was still only a matter of minutes before his backup would arrive and box me in.

"I was in a stolen Cadillac, with a dead body, a suitcase full of crack cocaine, and a wad of cash big enough to choke a buffalo. If they caught me, it would have been all over. And you need to understand, things were good. My life was way too posh to go down like that.

"I had to lose the cop and ditch the Escalade. I had to do it fast. I was running out of options with every passing second. Traffic was thickening. The walls were closing in. I saw a chance, and I took it.

"As I merged onto the freeway – no idea how fast I was going, but the petal was on the floor, and those Caddies ain't slow – as I merged, there was this old white sedan just ahead of me. I could have gone around 'er, but the cop would have done the same. Instead, I plowed into the sedan's left rear corner, sent it spinning into the guard rail.

"That idiot cop came flying up the ramp behind me, just like I knew he would. When the sedan careened off the rail, he tee-boned it, right there in the middle of the freeway. Crown Vic in the left center pocket, a perfect banked shot. I remember laughing like a loon, feeling the weight of that revolver laying across my chest and knowing I really was invincible.

"At the next exit, I slowed to a reasonable speed and parked under the freeway...just incase they had spun up a bird to look for me. The Caddie wasn't damaged much, probably could have gotten me home, but I dumped it right there, left the drugs and Twinkie, took the cash, and headed out on foot – right back to the original plan. By the time they untangled the mess on the freeway, I was long gone.

"The cops connected the Escalade to our rival gang. This would have been just a few weeks after Connie died, so I don't know if you'd remember at all, but it was a big story all over the news for a while. Several people were injured in that wreck, four of them were hospitalized. The mayor was under a lot of pressure to stamp out drug related violence in the city. We had to lay low for a while, but that other crew had to leave town altogether.

"The cops knocked over a few of their other houses, picked up a couple of their higher level dealers. They thought they were onto a major bust. By the time they figured out those guys were the small potatoes, the big potato," Alan pointed to himself, "was back in business, full swing."

Alan leaned back in his chair and took a deep breath, his eyes wandering as if considering how to proceed. Glen's mind grappled with the bizarre new picture Alan was painting of himself.

After a moment of consideration, Alan continued. "I had a girl back then, Shari. She was everything you would expect to see hanging off the arm of an up-and-coming drug lord – tall, blond, beautiful in a skin-tight, sexy sort of way. She was smart, too, which is why I kept her around. In that business you can get any girl you want, but you don't want just any hood rat or dope addled ditz.

"Shari was neither. She was as much a business person as I was. We made an arrangement – she would provide me with the class, credibility, and sex you can only get by having your very own super model. In return, I would feed her discreet but voracious coke habit.

"We were together five years. The arrangement worked out great for both of us...but that's all it ever was. I would have told you love is a sad sappy thing for weak fools who can't make it through life on their own. I thought I had no capacity for love whatsoever. Then Mandy was born.

"It was just shy of four years into our partnership. For the life of me, I'll never know how she came out so perfect, with as much cocaine as Shari was using at that time. I think God protected Mandy on purpose so He could get me. If she'd been born with problems, a 'crack baby' or whatever, I would have made Shari dump it somewhere and be done with the whole mess. But as it was, she came out beautiful...beautiful in a way I didn't know a person could be. I fell for that little smile, those baby, baby blues. I loved that little girl, and I almost felt like I was starting to love Shari.

"The only problem was she had a mean streak like nothing I've ever seen before. Or since. In those days, the only thing on God's green earth that scared me was Shari. I used to have a whopper of a scar right here,"

Alan touched his glass to his right cheek. "She got me with one of her stiletto heels.

"Just after Mandy turned one, Shari and I got into one of our huge fights – we actually had a name for fights like that, 'blitzkriegs' we called them. Shari was snorting a lot more coke than I thought was appropriate for the mother of my baby. She was totally blitzed that night, and we had both been drinking. I got her crying, which had never happened before. I took that to mean I had won." Alan looked up with a sad grimace he was trying to twist into an ironic grin. It didn't work, so he looked back down at his drink, continuing in an unsteady voice.

"She called me a hypocrite. I think I had a lump on my forehead where she had hit me with a lamp or something. I called her a crack whore, and a few less-pleasant things. She stormed out, bawling. I found some ice and a towel for my head, then flopped on the couch to bask in the glow of my victory.

"This part I remember precisely...I had just lifted my feet up to the arm rest at the far end of the couch when I heard an engine rev up. By the time I got to the window, Shari was peeling out of the driveway in my Corvette. She took Mandy with her." Tears welled in Alan's eyes.

"They didn't make it even three miles. She missed a turn, went off the road. The car hit a small tree. Didn't do much damage, but it stopped the car and might have knocked Shari out…or maybe she just passed out from the alcohol. It doesn't matter, I suppose, either way she didn't get out of the car.

"She hadn't been going that fast, but apparently the gas tank ruptured. There were sharp rocks at the edge of the road. I guess that's what did it. Anyway, a fire started…" An involuntary spasm gripped Alan's throat. His drink was empty so he took a long swig straight from the bottle. His hands trembled, but he managed it without spilling much. Then he sat for a long time just peering into the bourbon.

"They were killed in the wreck?" Glen ventured after a protracted silence.

"No." Alan said in a dead, flat voice. His eyes, bloodshot from tears and alcohol, wandered in a shocked despair from the bottle to Glen, then back to the bottle. "They were burned alive, Glen. Shari may have been unconscious, but Mandy would have been wide awake, shrieking and screaming, strapped into her car seat.

"I wasn't there, but I saw it – every night for years I dreamed it. Her perfect little fingers and hands burning as she screamed…And there is no one to blame but me. I burned my baby alive."

He shook then, trembled for what felt like a full minute. When his tremors subsided, he spoke again. "I destabilized after that, couldn't think at all. I turned my operation over to Mogs and just walked away.

"I was burning with rage. I wanted to kill anyone who was even a little bit responsible for what happened, but all that anger, all that venom just came back on me. I supplied the alcohol. I supplied the coke. I pissed her off. I let her go. I got her pregnant in the first place. I might as well have doused them in gasoline and roasted them myself.

"I didn't have the guts to kill myself. I tried, but couldn't. Even then I knew what I would find on the other side. Instead, I decided to destroy the person I had been. That would be almost as good as suicide. Also, I believed that our lifestyle – the drugs, the people we ran with – was as much responsible for their deaths as I was. I decided to destroy all that as well.

"About two months after the funerals, I pulled myself together. I stopped snorting coke, I quit drinking…This," he held up his empty glass, "is the first drink I've had in almost seven years. Anyway, this all happened in an election year. The District Attorney seat was very hotly contested, and the incumbent, our old buddy Gregory Anderson, was slipping in the polls. I saw an opportunity.

"I went to see D.A. Anderson, told him if he would get me immunity I could serve him up the biggest drug bust in the state's history. I learned a few things in that meeting – politicians are easier to manipulate than criminals, and they are just as corruptible if the incentive is big enough. Anderson bought it. Hell, he jumped at it, even invited me over to his house for dinner.

"He assembled twelve strike teams made up of state, county, and local police. Mogs was keeping me updated as to all of my cartel's operations, so I knew exactly where to send Anderson's teams. The day they struck, my suppliers were receiving a large shipment from the actual importers. Anderson's teams took down the whole chain. They seized millions of dollars in cocaine and made nearly a hundred arrests.

"His other teams raided all of my safe houses and distribution centers. I had squirreled away my cash elsewhere, of course. Anderson was uncannily effective. Our deal required that I would be 'killed' in one of the raids so that I could make a clean start and fade back into society. For this to be believable, there would have to be a few other casualties as well…you know, so as not to raise suspicions.

"The way it worked out, just about every one of my top guys, including Mogs, was killed. The deal Anderson and I made wasn't strictly legal. He wanted to make damn sure nobody figured out what he had done. As it turned out, he got so much good press from that operation his only opponent gave up, for all intents and purposes. Anderson won in a land slide.

"He set me up with a new name and a job in city records, got me an apartment – it was a dump compared to my old place, but no one was gonna come looking for me there. He even arranged for me to get a bit of surgery to remove that scar Shari gave me and to make sure if I ran into any of my old pals they wouldn't recognize me.

"The deal gave me immunity from prosecution for any crime I had committed in the past, so long as I stayed employed and didn't commit any new crimes. I stayed employed, stayed clean. But I had no direction, no friends, and the nightmares became much worse. You know about the dreams, don't you, Glen?"

Glen nodded, feeling as if he were in a dream right now.

Alan's voice was low, and hollow. "I told you I would see Mandy in my dreams, burning in her car seat. That was almost every night for weeks. Then the dreams began to change. Sometimes I would see the outside of the burning car, Shari and Mandy standing beside it, engulfed in flame, but just standing, looking at me, accusing and hating me with their eyes.

"I began to understand, these weren't just dreams, this was real, somehow, it was really Mandy…her spirit, or soul, or something. Not only that, she was still suffering. She wasn't resting in peace like I wanted to believe. She was still burning somewhere and she was pleading for me to help her.

"I had to do something. Destroying my past life wasn't enough. *I* was still alive and I still had sins to atone for. I decided the only thing I could do was live the best life a man could live. I would work with extreme dedication, give money to charity, bust my ass doing anything I could to make up for my past. I was going to outweigh my evil with good." He raised his eyebrows in a knowing look, a you-can-see-where-this-is-going look.

"I learned a lot about real estate and property values working in city records. I had a fat stack of Benjamins looking for a purpose, so I started buying properties. Turns out, all the same skills that made me good at hustling drugs also work for leveraging commercial real estate. Who would have guessed, right? Anyway, you came bumbling into my office with that hand typed flier about the Project, and the rest is history."

Alan rocked the bottle back and forth on the table, watching the slosh and swirl of the liquor. He gave a great, resigned sigh and took a long swig from the bottle. "It worked, for a while, I guess, trying to undo my evil past. Violent crime has dropped drastically in the city, and everyone tells me it's because of what we do here. There are fewer and fewer murders every year.

If that's a direct result of the work we've done, then we've saved more lives than I ever took. And if that's the measure by which I could buy back my soul, then I should have it free and clear.

"The problem is, it doesn't work that way, does it, Glen? The people I killed are still dead. They still hate me for killing them. The people whose lives we've saved don't even know we've saved them. But the spirits of those I killed, they still wait for me just beyond the veil.

"The more I realize this, the more I understand that the work I put into the Project was never really about me being noble or righteous. It was always only about trying to escape my sure damnation. For me, this Project is just as selfish as anything else I've ever done." He sat back in his chair, letting his head roll back until he was looking up at Connie's giant floating head. "And I guess the worst part is I am okay with that."

He seemed to think about this last statement for several seconds before continuing. "But that's not the case with you, is it, Glen?" he said. "You have been here these long years out of devotion, pure devotion, not to Constance Salvatore," he waved an arm in the general direction of her picture, "but to Connie. You have been trying to cling to her ghost while I've been trying to flee from mine.

"I need you to tell me about her, about *you* before

she died, about what happened that night. You Glen, are a pure soul. I don't know if I can ever understand that, but I want to. Do you get it? I want to.

"Tell me about that night, that last night. What happened out there that causes you such guilt? After what I've told you about me, what could you possibly have to hide?"

CHAPTER 16

THE BANQUETTE HALL HAD EMPTIED, the elegant contributors having left Connie behind for whatever entertainment completed their evening. Around the edges of the room, wait staff cleared tables, scooping glasses and flatware into large rubber tubs. They all avoided Alan's table.

Glen had sat transfixed through most of the monolog. He felt disoriented, lost. When he came here tonight, he knew Alan would try to get inside his head, would attempt to coerce him, by hook or by crook, to stay with the Project. But this was so far beyond anything he could have anticipated. The night had gone so weirdly awry. He had no idea how to process what he was hearing. Alan's invitation for him to speak came like the command of a hypnotist.

Without deciding to do so, Glen spoke. "I met Connie when I was eight. I guess I only really knew her six years, but when you're eight, years seem longer. She lived in one of the trailers just beyond the tracks. There was a path through the woods behind my house to that railway crossing at Holman Avenue, where Connie's shrine is. She would take that path to school every day, and I would wait so I could walk with her. The viaduct was a shortcut, but we had been warned to stay away from there, and we usually did.

From the day we met we were best buds. I don't know why, it just...clicked somehow. We pretty much spent every day together, doing each other's homework, exploring the woods, you know, what ever eight-year-olds do. As we grew a bit older, baseball was our favorite. I was a hell of a pitcher back then. She used to help me practice for little league – they didn't have baseball for girls, only softball, and she didn't want any part of that. I had other friends at school, but Connie was on a whole different level.

"Then we turned fifteen...Did you know we actually had the same birthday?"

"No, you never told me that," Alan said.

"Yeah, well, we did, born on the same day, in the same hospital, kinda crazy, huh?" Glen sipped his drink, the soda had gone flat, but the whiskey was still sharp. "There's something about turning fifteen...We had a party together. It was at my house because we had more room. Connie and I, we, uh...we always knew what the other was thinking, maybe because of how much time we spent together. I don't know, but it seemed like our minds had a connection. I think…I think that was the evening we fell in love. Or, at least we thought we did. What do fifteen-year-olds know of love, right?

"Anyway, about two days later, I asked her out on an 'official date' to go to the varsity baseball game. We always went to the games together, but never as a date. It scared me to death to ask her…I think that's the last brave thing I ever did. She said yes, of course. We met at the crossing like we always did. I took her hand as we walked to the game."

Tears were in his eyes. He looked up to keep them from falling. Above them, Constance Salvatore smiled down from the banner. "When I see that picture of her, it reminds me of the funeral, or the news paper articles, but it doesn't remind me of Connie. I can't really remember her face anymore, not what she really looked like…but I do remember how it felt to hold her hand.

"Sometimes I wake up from a dream of Connie and I can smell her hair, almost remember her face…still feel her small warm hand in mine, as if she were right there beside me. I lay very still for as long as I can, because as soon as I move or even just twitch, she slips away…that's the worst part, losing her as I wake." His eyes drifted away from the larger-than-life photo of a dark eyed girl who looked like dead Connie, but nothing at all like Connie while she was alive.

After an extended pause, Alan prompted, "You were on your way to the game..."

"Yeah, we met at the crossing. I held her hand to the game, through the game, and home again. We had never held hands before. I know this sounds...silly, but in all I've experienced since, I've never felt the thrill of love more acutely than I did while simply holding her hand."

Alan nodded, smiled.

"When we reached her house, I had to leave immediately," Glen continued, "to get home for some urgent chore. I walked her to her door, and just before I turned to leave, she leaned forward. I know she wanted me to kiss her."

Glen raised his hands in a gesture of frustration, as if to show something slipping from his grasp. "You don't...*can't* know fear of loss until you realize you have something to lose. I was so in love at that moment, and so scared, too. I didn't know. I..." His voice was lost, apologetic. "I was afraid if I kissed her she would...reject me? What if I kissed her only to discover that wasn't what she had in mind at all. I...I crumpled, panicked...I ran off and left her standing there, and cursed and damned myself all the way home.

"By the time I got there, I was so angry with myself, I resolved to go back to her house and give her that kiss, fear be damned. I would be bold and brave and kiss the girl." Glen accentuated his assertion with a broad upward swing of his right fist. His mocking smile turned and he slammed his fist on the table. "What a wretched yellow turd. If I could go back in time, I'd strangle myself for being such a worthless coward."

This seemed to catch Alan's attention more than anything Glen had said so far. His reddened eyes narrowed and he leaned a little closer in his chair. When Glen hesitated, Alan said, "You went back to her house?"

"Yeah, as soon as my chores were finished, I started off for her house again. Normally I would have taken the trail to the Holman Avenue crossing, but it was getting late – the sun was already setting – and I was in a hurry. I told you we knew each other's thought's, well, she must have read my mind that night. That's why she went to the viaduct, it has to be. There is no other explanation. She was on her way to see me...to get her kiss. If I hadn't been too damn scared to kiss her, she never would have been there in the first place.

"I had no idea she was out there, though, not at that point. As I approached the viaduct, I saw a man, early twenties maybe, standing in front of the opening. More were behind him in the tunnel. On any other night, I would have split as soon as I saw them, but that night I was on a mission. I was stoking up my courage to kiss Connie. I barely noticed they were there.

"When I reached the opening, the guy got up in my face. He told me to turn around and go back the way I came. Fear had already beat me once that day, and I felt it tightening in my chest again. There was no need to get beat up, I figured. I'd just go around the long way to Connie's house. I gave in almost instantly. Why not, right? The problem with fear is, once it has you on the run, it takes an enormous amount of courage to stop and face it.

"As I turned to leave, one of the other guys cried out. Then Connie screamed. He must have been holding his hand over her mouth. She probably kicked his shin or something and struggled loose for a minute. I knew it was Connie's voice, though I didn't see her.

"I spun around, but the man was directly behind me. His eyes were ice. He said, 'You didn't hear nothing. Turn around and walk away or I'll cut you open.' He had a knife, a switchblade, but I don't think that's what put me over the edge. It was his voice – completely devoid of emotion, like the guy was dead, and empty. His friends in the tunnel started yelling stuff like 'cut him up!' 'Cut off his nut sack.' He stepped toward me. I ran.

"I ran as hard and as fast as I could. I was going to get help. That's what I told myself. I'm not running away, I'm going to get help. Somewhere along the path,

I tripped over a root and went face first into a tree. I lay there until my parents found me later that night.

"And while I was sleeping, those men *beat* Connie, and *raped* her, and *killed* her." Glen emphasized each verb as he spoke, as much to torture himself as to inform Alan. "And when they heard a train coming, they dragged her up the embankment and tossed her on the tracks to cover their crime."

Alan started, "They would have killed you, too. There was nothing you could have…"

"Stop!" Glen snapped. "Don't you know how many times I've heard that? That's not the point. I wish I *had* died there that night. I would give up every single day I've lived since that night for the chance to die there instead of running away."

Glen stared at the table with his jaw clinched for a long time before speaking again. "I didn't tell anyone what I saw, not at first. I was ashamed, and...in shock, I guess. I remember those moments in front of the viaduct so clearly, but the weeks following...I don't remember a damn thing about them.

"Then they told me the investigation had concluded her death was accidental, that she had wandered onto the tracks, had somehow not noticed the train, and got herself killed. Can you believe that? I guess there wasn't much..." Glen shuddered, took a slow breath, and continued, "not much evidence to work with, but still...

"Anyway, I couldn't let that stand. I went to the police and told them what I had seen. I told them there were three guys in their early twenties, one of them in a leather jacket and close cut hair, and he had a knife. There wasn't much else I could tell.

"By that time her body had been cremated. The cops didn't believe me at first, thought it was some sort of grief thing, but I persisted and detective McGinnis agreed too look over her case again. He noticed that her shirt, jeans, sneakers and socks had all been recovered with the...her body, but no panties, no bra. How they overlooked this in the first place I don't know, but after this amazing discovery, they decided to take a look under the viaduct.

"They found some blood, some threads, a button that turned out to be from her shirt, and a...a...another item...but almost all of the evidence was gone, lost by passage of time. It wasn't until Monty Goglioni got himself shot with her underwear in his trunk that anyone really believed me. If it wasn't for that, we'd never have known who any of the killers were.

"So here's the deal, Alan," Glen was shaking now, "it was my cowardice that brought Connie to the tunnel that night, my cowardice that left her there to die alone, and my damned cowardice that let her killers get away. If you can claim credit for roasting your family, I get the credit for getting Connie raped, and killed, and run over by a train. Do you have any more questions?"

He had told this tale only a few times in his life, always with tears, always with intense shame, but this time there was anger, too, quite a lot of it. He hadn't ever intended to discuss this again, certainly not tonight, certainly not with this stranger he had thought he knew.

Yet the story did not seem to surprise Alan at all. He sat stone-faced for a moment, as if considering everything he heard, then said, "Yeah, Glen, just one more question. If somehow you got the chance to do it over, would you?"

Glen didn't answer, it seemed an utterly idiotic thing to ask. He looked to the door. a small crowd of stragglers had gathered there, donning their coats and saying their good-bye's. The rest of the room was empty.

"Of course you would," Alan answered his own question. "You've told yourself – fifteen times a day, every day, for the last eight years – that you'd give your life for the chance to do it over, to replay those few crucial minutes.

"I know because that's what I told myself every night, when I'd wake up screaming from one of my dreams. It became my mantra. Every time my guilt started creeping in, gnawing at my mind, I'd tell it,

'That's not me anymore. I've changed, I'm better, look at all I've done.'

"My guilt would say, 'Yes, but you can never undo what you did. You can never un-kill those kids. You can never un-rat Mogs. Then there's Mandy and Shari, you can never undo what you did to them.' And I would affirm with total unwavering earnest, 'But I would if I could! I would give it all for a chance to undo the evil I've done. I would give my life for one more chance, just one more chance!' And my guilt had nothing to say in reply, so it began to subside. The nightmares became less frequent. Eventually, they stopped altogether.

"For years everything was fine, great. I had forgiven myself and moved on. Then, two weeks ago, something happened. You came by afterwards, asked what was wrong. I'll tell you now what I couldn't tell you then. One last tale before we go our separate ways. I see you looking for the exit, Glen. Will you listen for just a moment longer before we are through with each other?"

Overhead, the giant floating head of Constance Salvatore watched over all. Glen felt completely untethered from reality. Everything he thought he had understood about his life after Connie was in flux, drifting. Alan had told him a story, and buried in that story were clues to a mystery he didn't want to solve. It had all happened so fast, this change in his friend, the revelation of Alan's sordid past. Something clicked inside Glen's brain, the way a vertebrae will sometimes pop back into place after being askew for years. Alan's crazy, horrible story, Glen's own confession of guilt, seemed to have jarred his mind loose.

The overhead lights dimmed as the room cleared. He and Alan were the only two still seated. A candle in their table's centerpiece flickered, casting shadows and yellow light across Alan's face as he spoke. He had launched into this final tale without Glen even realizing it. The man had always been a master of captivating with his words. Now, as he spoke, Glen's mind latched onto Alan's tale and traveled with his voice. He awoke in the dark with Alan, watching the events unfold as Alan spoke.

CHAPTER 17

ALAN WOKE IN THE DARK. The house was silent, much quieter than seemed right. It took him a minute to understand why. The power was out. All the little noises – the refrigerator, the heating system, the hum from his computer – they were all hushed. But something had awakened him, a sound. What had it been? He sat up in bed, listening intently.

Then he heard it again. A rattling, at the front door, the doorknob. Alan groped for his iPhone on the bedside table. He found it, but the display was blank, as if its battery were dead. Though the front door was one floor down and half a wing over, in the dead silence of the house, Alan heard it perfectly clear. It swung open. Footsteps clicked into his foyer. The door closed. The deadbolt *thunked* into its slot.

Rosalie was the only other person alive with a key to his house. Whoever was down there sounded like they were wearing high heels. Alan had never seen

Rosalie wear heels, had a hard time even imagining her wearing heels. And there was no way in hell she would show up unannounced at – what time was it, anyway? Pale moonlight streamed through the curtains on either side of his bed. No time read on his clock.

A state-of-the-art home security panel hung from the wall near Alan's bedroom door. It should have displayed either a red or a green LED. Neither shone. Alan slid open the nightstand drawer and fumbled through its contents, searching for the security system's panic button. He found it, but his hand brushed against something else, something heavy and hard and cold.

Downstairs, the heels *clacked*. Alan tracked the intruder's movements. They *clacked* into the formal dining room, paused halfway through. Silverware clinked. Was someone stealing his silver? It thumped softly back onto his tablecloth. He heard a soft, musical hum, and recognized it as a finger running around the rim of a crystal wine glass.

Alan had forgotten all about the panic button, not that it would have done him any good. He wrapped his fingers around the hard, cold grip of the old .357 magnum revolver and drew it from the drawer. He hoped it would once again be his good luck charm, his talisman, but now it did not make him feel invincible. Not at all.

The *clacking* became a *clicking* as the heels moved

from the dining room's hardwood floors to the kitchen's ceramic tile. The refrigerator door opened. Bottles clinked inside. A moment later the door closed.

Alan waited in the dark, mind racing. Had someone broken into his house to examine his silverware and the contents of his fridge? Someone in heels? Had she disabled his power, phone, and security to do so? He heard the wine cellar door creak open, and the muffled *tack...tack...tack* as the intruder carefully descended the wooden staircase. The door creaked closed behind her.

This was his chance. If she was in the cellar, he could creep down the back stairs and out to the garage. If he could make it to one of his cars, he'd high tail it to the nearest pay phone and call the cops. Sure, he had his pistol, but somehow he already knew that whoever walked his halls tonight, he did not want to confront her face to face, not alone, not in this dark silence.

He slid a foot out of bed, stealthy and slow. The instant it touched the floor, his bedroom doorknob clicked. Alan froze. A crack of light appeared around the door. It eased open, first half an inch, then an inch, then two. Alan raised the gun. He gripped it firmly with both hands, aiming for the spot in the opening where the intruder's chest would appear as soon as she stepped through.

The door drifted open a few more inches, then

stopped. The light spilling through was very dim, probably moon-glow from skylights in the hall. Alan thumbed the hammer back. The pistol trembled in his hands. He focused on his breathing, slow and steady, keep it together. His heart pounded in his ears. The revolver's front sight jumped with each beat.

A shadow moved into the doorway. It made no sound. This was not the clicking heels. They had returned to the kitchen, still moving at a leisurely pace. Whatever stood in his doorway was something else. It was short, less than two feet tall. Its head was slightly too large for its body. A creeping dread seeped into Alan's guts. Frozen spiders marched up and down his spine. He thought maybe he knew what stood in his doorway. He prayed to God he was wrong.

The heels clicked, and clicked, and clicked, through each room, pausing here or there, then resuming their meander, drawing ever closer to Alan. He knew that walk, that casual nonchalance. If he was right, if it was Shari strolling the darkened corridors of his house in the dead of night, then this had to be a dream. That was the only answer, the only reasonable explanation. The nightmares were back, which was okay. He could handle nightmares, had done it before.

But this didn't *feel* like a dream. Not at all. The thing in his door, the thing he refused to believe was Mandy, did not move, did not make a sound. The light

117

behind it brightened, just a bit, just enough to darken her outline. And those damn heels just kept clicking, clicking, clicking ever closer. Alan pushed himself all the way up in his bed, as far from the door as possible.

The clicking reached his bedroom. The door swung wide. Alan could no longer deny that the toddler standing in his doorway was Mandy. The silhouette that appeared beside her could only be Shari. He had always thought her body was stunning, and it hadn't lost a thing in the eight years since she died. In his nightmares, she had been burned – or burning – slowly being reduced to the charred skeletal relic Carl Withers had buried. Tonight, however, she was perfect, no hint of fire, no whiff of smoke.

She posed for him in the doorway – sliding a hand up the frame, cocking a perfectly sculpted hip – just long enough to be sure he saw her, then moved toward him, advancing in a slow, sultry strut. Her beauty was mesmerizing, which was horribly wrong. Alan tore his eyes away from her, focusing on his other visitor. Mandy's silhouette remained motionless. The blackness of her outline deepened in the brightening moonlight. Alan thought he might be able to make out her eyes, but wasn't sure he wanted to.

Shari stopped at the foot of his bed. "Look at *me*," she said, her voice a cold razor, the way it had always sounded just before one of their blitzkriegs.

Alan tried to speak. The words lodged in his throat.

Shari put her finger to her lips. "I'll talk. You listen," she said. "Nice house. I'm sure Mogs would have been impressed. You've really made something of yourself, haven't you? Mandy would have loved to play in the Jacuzzi tub...if you hadn't burned her alive."

Alan's eyes flicked to Mandy. Her outline wavered, as if eddies of scalded air rippled between him and her. He could see her eyes now, very clearly. They glowed a dull, angry red.

"It doesn't seem fair," Shari said, "that you should live in this luxury while we all roast in hell. Tell me, Carl – oh, I mean *Alan* – does it seem fair to you?" She came around the end of the bed, moving toward him in slow, measured steps.

"N-no. No, Shari. No, of course it's not f-fair, but, but...but what am I to do? I, I do the best I can, to to help...others, but I swear, if there was any way, any thing I could do to take it back, to undo what I did...if I could fix it, Shari, I swear on my life I would," Alan said. "I'd give anything to have one more chance, to start over and not fuck everything up like I did."

She glided forward, closing the distance between them until her face was only inches from Alan's. His pistol, which he had completely forgotten, pressed into her midsection. Heat poured off her body, baking

Alan's face and hands. Now he could smell her. She reeked of gasoline and sulfur.

"That's good enough for you, is it?" she asked, "that little lie you tell yourself? Well, I don't believe you. You wouldn't give this up. Not for me, not for Mandy. You have always been about you, only you, and no one else. You burned all of us and walked away clean. You live in a mansion and lie to yourself about what kind of man you really are. Well, I don't believe you. I want you to prove it."

"H-how?"

"You'll see," Shari said, smiling her wicked, playful smile. "You'll see soon enough. Mandy has a present for you."

Alan felt her hand close around his. He remembered the pistol, but only after she had it firmly in her grasp. She climbed onto the bed, straddling him, her face only half an inch from his. A new odor mixed with the sulfur and gasoline, the smell of burning flesh. Alan gagged on it. Vertigo swam in his head.

"I think I'll take this with me," she said. He felt the gun slip from his grasp, then felt a horrible dull thud as she crammed it into his crotch. "But I'll leave you something to remember me by."

"No, Shari, don't..."

She cut him off, pressing her lips over his. The other hand, the one not jamming a gun into his nuts, wrapped around the back of his head, pulling his face into hers. She forced her tongue deep into his mouth in a kiss that was, at first, ultimately sensual. Then, her tongue turned to the charred, rotting meat that it was. Her lips crumpled under the force of their kiss, disintegrating into dust and ash.

Alan tried to scream, but his mouth was sealed to Shari's. He retched against her stench and indescribable taste. Then she pulled the trigger.

CHAPTER 18

ALAN LOOKED UP FROM HIS empty tumbler, eyes wide, wondering, dazed, as if he were trying to decide whether he believed his own story. Then his eyes narrowed slightly, realizing Glen didn't believe it either.

"She didn't actually blow my nuts off," Alan amended. "The gun was snuggled up in there pretty tight, but she had the barrel pointed into the mattress. There's a hole straight through to the hardwoods under my bed.

"But a .357 Magnum kicks like a jackass. It punched me in the junk so hard I thought she had actually done it. Between that and her godawful kiss, I...I don't really know what happened. I think she dissolved into smoke, but I couldn't swear to it. I kind of fugued out for a while."

"Alan, you are out of your mind," Glen said. "That bug you picked up in the Philippines...this is all a fever dream or something..."

"God, I wish it were." Alan shook his head, then shuddered. "You'll see, in just a moment, you'll see. But let me finish, because this is the most important part. When I came to myself, sometime around sunrise I guess, I was covered in vomit and sweat. The room reeked of gasoline and smoke. My nuts were swollen up like a softball. There were still little flecks of burnt...meat, in my mouth." He heaved a deep sigh. "And I found something, the thing Mandy had left for me. It was laying on the floor in the doorway...where she had been standing." He pulled an odd wooden box from his suit jacket and placed it on the table.

Glen eyed the box. It looked like an incense holder, but larger, a little over a foot long and three inches square in width and height. The dark wood was carved and set with gems, abalone shell, mother of pearl. The stone and shell appeared not to be inlaid, but actually to have grown organically out of the wood. Fanciful gold hieroglyphs covered the lid.

Alan slid the box toward Glen. "I could tell you what's inside, but I've lost you. You think maybe my guilt's driven me around the bend, that I imagined all this? Let me tell you Glen, if that's true and you can prove it to me, I'll cut you a check right here for a cool million...but first, take a look in the box."

Glen eyed it warily. He picked up an unused fork and lifted the lid with it. A fragrant aroma of ancient oils and spices wafted from the box as the lid flopped open. He peered inside, then back at Alan. Glen suddenly felt a curious hope well up within him. A hope that maybe Alan actually had gone insane, that all the things he had said tonight were the mad ramblings of a delusional neurotic. If that were true, he could be helped, and all the craziness Glen had heard tonight would turn out not to be true.

"It's just a knife, Alan," he said, "what's it supposed to mean?" Yet, even as he spoke, he knew it was more than just a knife.

"Touch it."

"I'm not going to touch that thing. Tell me what it is."

"You have to touch it to understand, to know it's real. All I know...all I can say in words is this— You see these characters here?" Alan pointed to the top row of lettering on the lid. "I have sent scanned images to linguistics professors around the globe. No one has been able to translate them, or even identify their origin. That second row of letters is different. An antiquities professor in Damascus figured that part out. It's an old Assyrian dialect which cannot be directly translated but roughly says something like, 'The Time Weaver's Gift.'" He paused to let that sink in, then added, "It's a second chance, Glen."

Glen looked back into the box. The dagger's blade

was double edged, almost ten inches long. An etched ivy pattern twined along its full length. At the blade's base, a pair of boar's tusks curved out and upward, forming the guard. The handle was a freakish amalgamation – various bits of bone and fur and shells, human and fish teeth, ribs from some small rodent, a tuft of rabbit fur, a bit of oyster shell, flecks of sand and smooth slips of coral – all bound together in gold solder and wrapped in a thin film of snake skin.

"What do you mean, 'second chance'?"

"Glen, just touch the knife."

Glen gave him a curt smile and stuck one finger into the box. As soon as his finger entered, however, everything changed. The thing in the box called out to his mind. And his mind answered.

Without intending to do so, Glen wrapped all four fingers around the handle. Before he had a chance to wonder why he had done so, sharp prickles exploded inside his head. Blackness consumed his vision. The feeling was similar to passing out from standing up too quickly.

A sheer wall of sensation crashed into his brain. A rush of images, senses, sounds inundated his mind. He felt and heard the soft thud of his sneakers on a forest trail. He smelled moist loam and moss, heard crickets, felt the breeze on his face as twilight filtered through the canopy of oak leaves. He also felt, more acutely than all else, the fluttery pounding of his heart, the apprehension that caused his steps to falter and the anticipation that drove him on. Adrenalin and endorphins pounded with the blood in his veins, and he felt that, too.

Intellectually, he knew he was sitting at a table in a banquette hall, but all of his senses demanded he was on the path to Connie's house. It was not a vision, but his own memories. He could feel them being drawn from some seldom visited chasm of his mind, the way one would draw water from a deep well.

As he rounded a corner on the path, a new scent joined the earthy forest aroma, the distinct smell of creosote. The path turned again and suddenly the stone arch of the viaduct loomed directly in front of him. Its mouth was dark. Within, broken glass glimmered in the dying light. Graffiti glared from its walls. The creosote smell was much stronger here, as was the heavy smell of the tunnel's dark dampness.

The memory shifted suddenly, blurred, and froze, but as it did Glen recognized a figure standing in the archway. The tingly popcorn explosions filled his head again and he became aware of a new terrifying perception. The knife thing in his hand was somehow alive, pulsing. The tiny bits of dead things comprising its handle squirmed in his grasp. It had been directing this memory, but now its intent changed. It directed something else. Glen suddenly felt an overwhelming urge to plunge the blade into his heart. The living dagger *wanted* to be buried in his heart.

Glen startled, jarred back to reality. He released the knife, dropping it into its box. He was breathing heavily, sweating, trembling a little bit.

"Real enough?" Alan asked.

"What the hell was *that*?"

"Would you really give your life for a chance to change the past, Glen?"

Glen stared at the knife. It stared back at him. It had imparted to him, along with the intensified memory, a kind of knowledge, an understanding of what it was, what it could do. All Glen's mental gatekeepers, which normally would have rejected paranormal nonsense, had been hog-tied and thrown into the closet. What was revealed to him was ridiculous, absurd even. But he found it impossible not to believe. The memory of the knife in his hand vanquished any doubts he had.

Glen looked at his palm, then up to Alan. "If I show my willingness to make it right by taking my own life, with this blade, by killing myself…then Connie gets to live?" He paused, "No. No, I'll go back…"

"…and get the chance to do it over." Alan finished for him. He was smiling now, not a happy smile, but the smile of a man watching another muddle through a bewildering rite of passage that he, himself, had recently endured.

Glen's mind swarmed with questions, *How can this be? Is it real? Does it work? How does it work?* but the knowledge from the knife squashed them all.

"You know it's real, don't you?" Alan said. "You're trying to reject it but you can't. I can see it in your eyes."

Glen felt as if he were sliding down a greased chute. There was an inevitable conclusion, a conclusion he absolutely must reject, but he could find no ground for doing so. Then, his mind latched on to something, a question.

"If it is true, where's Shari?" he asked.

"What?"

"If this thing is real – and if that story you told me about you being a, a...a drug lord – if that story is true, and if this blade does what you say it does, you would have used it already. Shari would be with you now. So where is she?"

Alan stopped smiling. "You always were too smart for your own good." He sighed, then said, "That line of logic breaks down for two reasons. First, the decision I would have to change to put me on the upward path occurred before I became a drug lord. If I went back and changed it, I never would have met her.

"Second, and more to the point, Shari was right. When you cut away all the fluff and happy hand shakes, all I am is selfish. I have worked too long and too hard. I can't just throw it all away. I'm a respected pillar of this community, a captain of industry. I'm wealthy, I have many classy ladies I can take out for a night on the town, any time I like. Life is good, Glen, way too good. And I know, if I had made honest decisions when I was young, I never could have accomplished all this.

"I told myself, over and over again, that I would make things right if I could. But now that I can, it turns out that all I am is a selfish liar. I hate that about myself...but not enough to change it." He clasped his hands together on the table and looked into them as if trying to catch a glimpse of something that was slipping away. "When I was young, I didn't expect to end up like this. In some ways it's better than I expected...in a lot of ways it's much worse. But I'm not willing to risk it all for a chance to make it right.

"I don't regret what I've done. I regret what I've become...and even that's not a satisfying sorrow, because if I wanted to I could change it. But I won't." Alan looked like some grievously wounded animal, too far gone to save, but still a long way from dead.

Glen wondered what the most merciful coarse of action might be. "What was your decision," he nodded at the knife, "the one you see when you touch that thing?"

"That doesn't matter now, Glen, not at all. It's in the past, *and it's going to stay in the pas*t. The real question is you. Are *you* willing to give up your life for the chance to relive those few minutes?"

Again, Glen did not answer, but this time the question did not seem so stupid.

"You need to understand, Glen, when I say 'give it up,' I mean give it *all* up. If you do go back, if you try to save Connie, you *will* die. You said there were three grown men, with knives. We know what they did to Connie. What do you think they'd do if a fifteen-year-old kid shows up and tries to spoil their fun?

"If you die back then, you and I will never meet...though you might not mind that now. You'll never meet that girl over in Oakville. You'd be walking away from every thing that is your life."

"Maybe that's okay, if Connie survives..." He wasn't fully convinced of this, or of anything else for that matter, but his hand was already moving toward the box.

Alan grabbed his wrist and glared at him. "How can she be worth it, Glen? Your whole life for some little girl?"

"Because she is what my life has been about. All the time, all the energy I spent on the Project...I didn't do it as some misguided attempt at self redemption, Alan. I did it for Connie. And when it started to be about me, and you, and the damn politicians, I knew it was time to walk away.

"But you kept me here. I thought you were trying to help me, but all this time I was propping up your feeble attempt to outrun the selfish coward you used to be. Or still are, I guess." He looked at Alan, trying to read him.

"And what about your sister?" Alan asked, almost pleaded. "Who'll be around to look after Sophia if you get yourself killed?"

When he said her name, Sophia, all the pieces fell into place. An odd species of hate ignited somewhere deep in Glen's chest, and a dawning revulsion. This man whom he had loved and worshiped throughout his entire young adulthood had been not just a fraud, but something much worse.

Three things he had said during his wild confession flashed into Glen's mind, *I don't suspect we'll see each other again after tonight, not with what I'm about to say,* and, *our lives are intertwined, more so than you know,* and, *the sedan careened off the rail, the cop tee-boned it, right there in the middle of the freeway. Crown Vic in the left center pocket.*

"It was Sophia, wasn't it?" Glen asked. His voice was flat, but his heart buzzed in his chest like hornets trapped in a jar. "The sedan you hit to cover your ass, that was my sister's car?"

Tears stood on Alan's lids, his eyes red. Glen guessed the alcohol had more to do with that than anything else, but it still unnerved him to see it. Alan met his eyes for a moment, then looked away. He reached toward the bottle again, but Glen grabbed it.

"Alan?" he demanded.

"I didn't know who it was, Glen," he said. "I didn't know you then, I..." he sighed, staring into his empty tumbler. "I think it was Sophia."

"Let go of my wrist," Glen said. Alan's hand relaxed and slid to the table.

"Glen..." Alan started.

"Haven't you said enough?" Glen snapped. He grabbed the box and stood. The room wavered as he did, and seemed to spin. After a second it stilled. Glen shook his head, staring at the older man. "I'm going for a walk, Alan. I really liked the person you pretended to be. I think I'll miss him."

"Glen, wait a minute," Alan said. "When you get to where you're going, if you make it, if you manage to save Connie, maybe you could look me up...maybe help straighten me out?"

"Connie isn't going to die on that viaduct, not this time. As for me, surviving isn't a priority. And even if I do, I hope to God I never meet you."

Glen turned and walked across the empty banquet

hall without looking back. Alan sat alone at the table as his footsteps receded into the dark, wondering what would become of him if Glen used the knife.

CHAPTER 19

GLEN STEPPED OUT OF THE banquet hall onto Ninth Avenue. It was late Autumn and a swirling wind chased brittle leaves to some unknown destination. Glen followed, his destination was the same. This time felt old, and it no longer seemed as if he belonged in it. The idea that this knife might transport him to some other time seemed simultaneously ludicrous and undeniable.

He tried to drink deeply of all his senses. If this was to be his last night in this world, he wanted to make it memorable. For the first time in all his years walking this street, he noticed the large flat foundation stones of these old buildings, stones that were too stately and massive to have been quarried any less than a hundred years ago. He ran one hand along the dull spear-points of a wrought iron fence, points worn smooth and shiny from a century of passing hands.

The moon loomed huge and yellow on the

horizon, like an ancient eye peering over the rim of the world, mildly wondering what he might do. A dry-leaf potpourri hung in the air, gathering around him from the city's maples and aged oaks. He also smelled the thin film of time that lay on the city – oil and exhaust, soot, mold and dust, soft masonry.

The knife, in its case, sang to him, its voice nothing more than the whisper of a moth's wings inside his head. He wanted to distrust the relic's power, but the longer he held it the harder it was to deny. It felt solid in his hands, while the rest of his world seemed thin, used up. He clasped it more tightly to his side, and in doing so felt an irregularity on the underside of the box. He turned it gently over to discover a brass tag riveted to the bottom of the case. Stamped across it in simple letters was, "Samir's Curiosities."

When he reached an intersection the wind shifted. The leaves turned right on Fischer Boulevard and Glen followed. To the south, still half an hour out of town, a train let out its long, sad wail. The only other sounds were the *tic tic tic* of leaves who had served their purpose and been discarded, and the occasional odd voice of the wind. It shifted again when he reached Tenth Avenue, back to the course it had previously pursued. Again Glen followed, watching the leaves run away from him into the dark.

Tenth Avenue and Fischer was considered the

antique district, though much of what was sold there was worthless junk less than twenty years old. Glen considered these shops just a bunch of pretentious second-hand stores. Varieties of glass and china and furniture decorated their display windows, but their interiors were filled with nothing but old clothes, nick-knacks, and trinkets from the seventies and eighties.

As he followed the fleeing leaves past these carnivals of garbage, he heard a faint buzz, then a pop. A small neon sign came to life and casually announced one of these stores was open. Above the neon, a dark wooden sign read, in gold letters, "Samir's Curiosities." Light blinked on inside the shop. Glen heard the deadbolt in the solid oak door slide open.

The box hummed, buzzed in his hand. He stood a moment longer looking at that door, then it opened just a crack. Fragrant air wafted out into the street – aloes, cinnamon, myrrh, cloves, incense and oils. Glen imagined this is how the burial preparations for a pharaoh would have smelled.

He stepped under the archway, into the shop. His first impression was that Samir's Curiosities was a gallery or museum rather than another Tenth Avenue junk store. The isles were wide, and few in number. Rather than shelves, they were comprised of display cases and pedestals. There were no clothes hanging on racks. There were no bins to rummage through. Each and every piece on display had its individual place, and each was illuminated by its own miniature spotlight.

Glen was aware of the dark man behind the counter, but for a moment was captivated by the various glimmering artifacts. It struck him that these were true antiques, yet they looked newer than anything else he'd seen on Tenth Avenue. Alabaster things with lapis lazuli eyes, goblets, brass oil lamps, a sexton, a ring, a rifle, a compass, a rough leather-bound book – which was actually hand written, as if it pre-dated the printing press – and several things he didn't recognize, all glowing under the soft spot lights. Age had settled thick on the floors and walls here, as it had everywhere on Tenth, but the artifacts themselves were untouched by it.

"May I help you?" The man at the counter looked up from a large open book in which he had been writing. He placed the gold gilded quill into its inkwell with the slow deliberateness of a man who has complete command of his surroundings and is neither startled nor rushed by any circumstance.

"Do you recognize this?" Glen asked, placing the box on the counter.

"Ah, yes," he said. A subtle smile softened his lip, as smooth as melting butter. He was undoubtedly of middle-eastern descent, with olive skin and a tight cap of thick black hair. His suit was black silk, deep as the midnight sky, and without wrinkle or any sign of wear. He spoke with the cool confidence of a mafia kingpin, and the charm of a sultan at a banquette.

"Again the knife returns to me," he said with mock bewilderment. "It tells you all that is necessary if you just grasp the handle, yet each new owner seeks me out." He stretched out both hands like a benevolent, indulgent father. "What question do you have that the knife has not already answered?"

Glen hesitated. The man's reaction confirmed all that the knife had shown him. Hearing this, he realized he had no question to ask, at least not about the knife. He could pretend to disbelieve while it was safely tucked away in its box, but if he grasped the handle...just the thought of touching it brought its reality crashing back into his brain.

He did not need to ask about the reality of the knife. There were other answers he still needed – the world as he had known it was slipping away – but he had no idea what the questions were. Eventually, one came to him, "Are you the 'Timeweaver?'"

"The knife is mine," Samir answered. His demeanor remained as smooth as oil, but this question clearly annoyed him. "That silly box, though, some fool who fancied himself to be a poet made that. I am not a 'timeweaver.' I am Samir, a simple scribe. I neither create nor direct the events of time. I only record them.

And furthermore, that knife is not a 'gift.' It is a curse…as all who have owned it can attest."

Samir opened the lid, revealing the knife. It was both beautiful and hideous, and jolted Glen again with the memories. Samir caught the determination in Glen's eyes.

"Young man," he began with the brashness of an Egyptian elder, "for thousands of years this curse has passed from one broken man to the next. Hundreds of men have held it, and none, not *one*, has ever used it." The finger he had been pointing at Glen's chest he now held up to indicate the 'one'. He still maintained his impeccable poise, but fire burned in his eyes, an old angry fire.

Glen understood he had been set up to ask 'why not,' that the answer was already in the mouth of this beautifully preserved antique, and that he probably didn't want to hear it, but he asked anyway.

"Because," Samir answered, "you are all a silly fickle race of naïve fools and squanderers. Because of all that there is, only you people are blessed with the gift of choice. Every other thing in the universe performs its function precisely as it was designed to do. They have no option, no ability to deviate. But you, you," he was shaking his open hands in front of him toward Glen, "you get to choose, to decide if you will behave as you ought, or otherwise.

"Yet, you give no more thought to your gift of choice than you give to the circulation of your blood. You choose and choose and choose and never stop to think, 'Is this a good decision?' You put less thought into your life's work or your life's mate than you do into which flavor of ice cream to eat at the ice cream parlor.

"And when, as if by a miracle, you discover that you have made a foolish choice, you whine and wail. You cry in the night, 'Oh, God, how could I have been so foolish? If I could only have one more chance, I would choose right the second time around, I promise I would!'

"And then I, *Samir,* who have no ability to choose, no option to do otherwise, am burdened with the task of recording all your stupid decisions," with a broad sweep of his hand he indicated the large book in which he had been writing, "and not only the decisions, I must also record all your silly little 'if only' prayers, all your pathetic pleas.

"As you might imagine, this labor became wearisome. So I sought an audience with the One who does weave time and I presented my case before Him. I argued that the right of choice was far too powerful a thing to be bestowed on a people as immature and simple as you. I presented as evidence the chaos and destruction that typifies and defines your existence. I

140

presented the myriad volumes I have composed that contain nothing other than the plea, 'I would give my life for a second chance.' I concluded by stating that choice was a power far beyond the feeble capacity of the terrestrial beings He had created, and that He must revoke the right of choice in order to restore contentment and peace to His creation."

Once again, the thought occurred to Glen that this was utterly absurd. None of it fit the logic he thought he knew. But before the thought had a chance to fully materialize, it was squashed by the aura of the room, by Samir's eyes, by the knife in his peripheral vision. All the barriers to accepting this new paradigm had been anticipated and set aside by the sheer supernaturalness of his surroundings.

Samir waited for a response. Glen asked, "How did he answer your charge?"

"With this." Samir took the knife from its box and placed it on the counter, closer to Glen. He could feel the pulsing power of the blade and the rush of sensuous memory.

"He told me, 'I have given them choice because it suits my purpose. I have given you the task of recording their choices because that, too, suits my purpose. Most choose poorly, as you have clearly shown, but there are those who choose well. How are we to know which is which unless we let them all choose?'"

"'This,' He told me, 'will be our wager. If one man in a thousand has the strength of character to lay down his life in order to make right what he made wrong, then I will have won. If however, not one in a thousand will die to right his wrongs, then your charge will be considered valid.' And He presented me with this, which I in turn presented to Abed-Nahor, over thirty-five hundred years ago.

"It has passed through the hands of over seven hundred men, great men of the earth, those of renown and valor, those of the strongest character. Each and every one of them made some poor choice which they claimed they would lay down their life to rectify, yet not one of them were actually willing to do so."

Samir's voice had raised bit by bit over the coarse of his explanation, growing emphatic, querulous. He took a breath and studied Glen's eyes. When he spoke again, his voice had softened to an almost dismissive tone. "And now it has come to you."

"What are the stakes?" Glen concentrated on maintaining eye contact with Samir, though the knife pulled his gaze toward it. His palm itched to grasp its handle again.

"The stakes?" Samir seemed surprised. "Ha! The stakes are simple. If He wins, if a man actually uses the knife, I have to start over. I have to rewrite all the history from the point at which he changed his original

142

decision...a monumental task. You, for example, if you were to go back, would cause me to rewrite every choice and action of every person on earth for the past eight years. One minor deviation in the stream of time will reroute its entire course."

"And if you win?"

Samir settled back a little, his subtle smile returned. "He has to start over, from the very beginning. He must recreate mankind without the ability to choose."

"That's pretty heady stuff for a simple scribe."

Samir's smile deepened.

Glen surveyed the shop again. Over seven hundred bits of history, some as old as thirty-five hundred years, glinted and glowed on counters and pedestals and cases. A few pieces appeared to be from the modern era. A chrome plated, snub nosed revolver – a .357 magnum – gleamed in the display case under the counter. On the ledge behind Samir, dangling from an alabaster hand, hung Glen's silver cross, the one that had belonged to Connie.

Samir saw Glen's eyes travel from the revolver to the cross. In explanation of his collection, Samir said, "Every man who returns the knife unused loses a little piece of his soul."

Glen thought of Shari burning in eternity, of Alan as an empty old man in a dark room and as a young dangerous drug lord, of Rochelle and Sophia and the thousands of lives he had touched through the Project, and finally of Connie who…who what? He didn't know how to define or characterize her. He truly couldn't remember much, except that when he was fifteen he had loved her and he hadn't been alive since she died.

He wrapped his fingers around the knife's handle and shuttered with its energy.

Samir laid his hand on Glen's. "Young man," he said, his voice consoling. "The knife was not meant to come into your hands. This curse should never have fallen upon you. Take no offense, but you are not one of the great men. This burden weighs heavy upon one such as you. Perhaps you should return it to me. I will make sure it finds a proper owner."

Samir's grip tightened, and Glen was suddenly certain Samir would try to forcibly take the knife from him. He held it firmly and said, "No."

"Of all the princes and moguls throughout these long eons," bitter cynicism gilded Samir's smooth words, "surely you, a commoner, do not have the strength of will to wield this knife?"

"I need to...to think."

"Do you really?" Samir's voice now dripped with contempt. He reached under the cabinet, withdrew what looked like a leather bound encyclopedia, and flopped it onto the countertop. "Eight years, Glen McClay. Eight years of promises. 'Dear God, please let me have a second chance, let me do it over. I'd do anything, I'd die for just a chance to save her. Please God let me die instead of her.' Does that sound familiar? I have recorded that exact prayer in excess of three-thousand times — *three-thousand times* — yet now you need to think about it? You are wasting my time. Leave the knife and go."

"Things have changed since then." The knife pulsed in Glen's palm. The shop's spice scents had been replaced by moss and mud and creosote. He heard the faint echo of laughter, the faint echo of a scream. "This is a decision, a *choice*, Samir. Are you suggesting I should make a choice of this significance without thinking it through?"

Samir's eyes softened. The cynicism in his smile melted to bemusement. "I suppose not," he conceded. "But perhaps you should do your thinking at your sister's house. The passage I was writing, just before you interrupted, concerns her."

Glen craned his neck to see what Samir had written. His letters were beautifully formed, but certainly not English, perhaps not even a human language. "What about my sister?"

"I think you will want to be with her tonight, that is all," Samir continued. "And I think by the morning you will realize that this knife is not for you." He released Glen's hand. His smile was now warm, almost grandfatherly. "Return it to me in the morning," a slight nod, "and I will give you a full refund. That is not an offer I have ever made before."

Glen's eyes went to Connie's crucifix dangling from the alabaster hand. "I...appreciate that. I..." But he didn't know what else to say.

"Now," Samir said, "if you will excuse me, I have quite a bit of writing to do." With that, he returned to his journal. Glen placed the knife in its box. The forest smells and Connie's voice dissipated when he released its handle. As he walked out of Samir's Curiosities, Glen heard the old Egyptian's feather pen scratching line upon line of history into his ledger.

CHAPTER 20

MUFFLED VOICES DRIFTED UP FROM the house below. Dale had brought over pizza and salad. He and Sophia had just been cracking into their second six pack, Bud Light, and playing Jenga at the kitchen table when Glen returned. Glen had said howdy and goodnight as quickly as possible. Dale and Sophia seemed plenty pleased to be rid of him.

Now, Glen lay on his bed, staring at the dark ceiling, trying to sort out his scattered thoughts. He drifted near the edge of sleep, head so full of conflicting ideas and images it seemed impossible to hold on to any one of them long enough to get the sense of it. He needed to speak to his mentor, but his mentor was a fraud. And worse than a fraud.

As he slipped into an uneasy slumber, the thing in the box, the Timeweaver's wager, poured remembered sensations into his brain. Feet pounded on the forest path. A giant maple leaf drifted in a slow spiral through the canopy. Echoes of water splashing under the viaduct. Hot skin in the summer sunshine. Cool damp darkness in the tunnel under the tracks. Everything perfect, nearly perfect, not perfect at all. Below all this – or behind it – something was terribly, terribly wrong. In his dream, Glen coughed, only he wasn't Glen anymore, he was Connie, and when she coughed, flecks of foamy blood speckled an iron rail and the stones beneath it.

A racket and clatter startled Glen out of his doze. In the kitchen, the Jenga tower had toppled, crashing across the table and floor. Glen expected a torrent of raucous laughter to follow. Instead, something else crashed in the kitchen, much louder this time. Glass shattered. Glen was up and out of bed, dashing for the door.

Then he heard the scream. It sounded like iron wheels on iron rails, locked down, braking to stop but having no luck at it. It sounded more animal than human, carrying on longer than Glen would have thought a human could scream.

He was taking the stairs three at a time when the scream stopped, replaced by a ragged sucking in of air. He heard Dale's panicked chanting, "holyshit, holyshit, holyshit..." Then Sophia screamed again, just as Glen rounded the corner into the kitchen. She was lying on the floor under the toppled table, back arched, arms splayed, legs kicking. Dale stood over her, both hands clamped onto the hair at the back of his head. The blood had drained from his face to the point that it looked blue. "...holyshit, holyshit, holyshit..."

Glen ran to his sister. Dale bolted for the front door. The scream cut off abruptly as Sophia's teeth snapped closed like a sprung bear trap. *Oh, God, her tongue...*Glen thought, scooping her head into his arms. "Dale!" he screamed, "come back here!"

The front door hung open. Tires squealed. Dale's car lurched out of the drive backwards, across the street toppling the neighbor's mail box, shifted in to drive, and shot off down the street.

Glen cradled Sophia's head in his lap, protecting it from pounding into the floor as she convulsed, protecting it from her flailing left arm. Blood foamed through her teeth as she moaned. She must have struck her face before he got to her. Blood ran freely from both nostrils. Her eyes were peeled wide but showed only white. She was slick with sweat.

Glen cooed to her. "It's okay, Sophia. You're okay. I've got you. It'll be over soon. You'll be alright..." His eyes flicked between the open front door and Sophia's cell phone, both too far to reach with out leaving his sister. Her left wrist cracked him in the side of the head, hard enough to make lights flash behind his eyes. The arm dropped, then swooped up in the same arc. Glen dodged the blow the second time around.

The seizure continued. Her teeth remained clamped shut, lips peeled back in a hideous snarl, jaw muscles hard as stones beneath her cheeks. The moan turned to a high keening wail that bubbled through the blood in her nose. At one point, Glen saw someone on the street craning her neck to peer through the open front door, but when he called out for help, the lookyloo scurried off.

Moments later, Dale ran back through the door, still chanting, "shit, shit, shit, I'm sorry, shit, I'm sorry, shit..."

"Dale," Glen yelled, "call an ambulance."

"I did, Glen," he said, panting. "I called 'em, I'm so sorry, shit, I'm sorry, Sophia."

He stood nearby, still trembling, white-faced, grasping his hair. "What can I do?"

"Just..." Glen dodged another left flail, "just hold her hand, man, hold her hand."

Dale took one hesitant stutter-step forward, then resolutely knelt and grasped her arm. A second later he had her hand in both of his. Taking his cue from Glen, he cooed and calmed her with his voice.

The seizure lasted just under six minutes, though it seemed much longer. By the time the first ambulance arrived, she had gone completely limp. The paramedics managed to rouse her enough to determine her brain function was not likely to be impaired. She slid in and out of awareness through the remainder of their examination.

Her tongue was intact, but she had chipped a tooth and put a large gash on the inside of her right cheek. The paramedics applied a cross of white tape over the bridge of her nose. It probably wasn't broken, they said, though she should have the doctor look at it. Bruises had already started to spread beneath her eyes. Both would be ringed in dark purple by morning. That and a few other bruises were the extent of her injuries. The paramedics recommended recovery at home, as long as someone would be there to keep a close eye on her for the next twenty-four hours. Glen and Dale both assured them that Sophia would not be left alone.

When the light show was over, Glen and Dale cleaned off the blood that remained on Sophia's face and neck, then helped her to bed. Throughout this, Sophia remained in a semiconscious state. She only once woke enough to grasp her situation, at which point she cried and cursed them both and told them not to look at her and to leave her alone. Then she drifted off again.

Dale held her hand while Glen got a chair from the kitchen. When he returned he told Dale to go home, check back in the morning.

"You ain't gonna tell her I ran out, are you?" Dale asked. "Do you think she'll know?"

"You're going to tell her, Dale," Glen said softly. "You're going to tell her it scared the shit out of you and you ran away."

"Yeah, I guess I will," Dale said.

"Otherwise you'll spend the rest of your life wishing you told her," Glen said, taking a seat in the chair and taking Sophia's hand from him. "But you also came back, and you called the ambulance. And I will tell her that. And I'll remind her of it every time she forgets."

Dale managed a grateful, bewildered smile. "That was some fucking terrifying exorcist shit, man."

"You are *not* going to tell her that."

"No, I guess I won't," he said. "Is this because of...you know." He traced a line along his forehead, mirroring Sophia's scar.

Glen nodded. "She had a couple seizures the year it happened, but none since. They put her on pills for it."

"Does this mean she's going to start having them regular?"

"I don't know, man," Glen said. "I guess she'll need to see her doctor...but good luck getting her to go."

"Why?"

"The doctor will insist on taking her drivers license – she lost it for a few years after her accident. Also, no swimming, bathing, or showers without someone around to look out for her until they are confident she won't have another seizure."

"Shit," Dale said. "I don't think I want to be around when she gets that news."

"She'll give up the license," Glen said, "but she'll do as she pleases on all other fronts. We'll need to be available to help her whenever she lets us. You and me is all she's got, Dale."

"And you're leaving," Dale said. "Heading off to college like you should have done five years ago."

Glen looked at the inside of his hands. He could still feel the weight of the knife against his palms, and the strange, wriggling texture of its handle. It called to him. He had a strong urge, even now, to leave Sophia just long enough to run up to his room and retrieve it. "I don't know if I'm leaving, or not," he said, finally. "Don't know if I can now."

"No, dude, you *have* to go. It would fucking kill her for you to stay on her account. You know that, right?"

Sophia was snoring softly now. Glen brushed her sweat drenched bangs down over the scar. "Yeah, I suppose I do."

"She told me this might happen someday," Dale said. "I guess I better get my head straight so I can deal with it if it happens again. I'm sure I can. If you know what's coming, it's easier to prepare for it."

Glen nodded, thinking that those may be very wise

words indeed. "Thank you, Dale, for coming back, but you need to go now. You can stop by in the morning, but I guess once she gets a look at her face, she's not going to want to see anyone until the bruising goes down."

"Are you going to sit up with her all night?"

"Yes, Dale. I will."

"What about the mess in the kitchen?"

"Leave it."

"You sure?

"Yes, Dale, good night."

"Good night," Dale said, and this time, when he left, he closed the door.

CHAPTER 21

GLEN SAT BESIDE SOPHIA. EVENTUALLY he dozed. In his dreams, bubbles of blood formed and popped in Sophia's nostrils. Her left arm swung and flailed. The inhuman scream reverberated inside Glen's skull. But the screaming wasn't Sophia. He was very used to hearing Connie scream in his dreams, but it wasn't her, either. It was iron wheels, locked and skidding down iron rails. It was now Connie's arm that flopped, not in a rigid convulsion, but in a loose and feeble groping. Glen lived this dream from within Connie's mind, experiencing it as she had.

She coughed. Foamy blood stippled the side of the iron rail. Red droplets burned bright as embers in the locomotive's glaring single beam. Her left arm glowed in angelic radiance under that intense light. Pebbles and dust jumped like flees around the vibrating rails and ties. The shriek intensified, the light burned ever brighter, brighter, brighter.

Glen opened his eyes, winced, and raised his left arm up to shield them. A shaft of bright morning sunlight streamed through a gap in the curtains, landing full on his face. After a second to remember where he was, he leaned forward and closed the curtain.

Sophia lay on the bed exactly as they had placed her, nostrils flaring slightly with each inhalation. Dark golf-ball-sized patches spread outward from the corner of each eye. The white tape cross on her nose reminded Glen of Connie's cross, dangling from an alabaster hand in Samir's Curiosities. *Every man who returns the knife unused loses a little piece of his soul.*

And how much of his soul does he lose if he uses the knife? Glen wondered. He wouldn't leave Sophia like this...not to chase some crazy fantasy about saving Connie. How could he? And what could he hope to accomplish by going back – if going back was even possible?

What would have happened that night if he had charged into the tunnel instead of running away? Alan was right. The three thugs in the tunnel, who had no compunction what-so-ever about brutally murdering Connie, would kill him just as readily. His only shred of hope was that they would be distracted enough with him that Connie might have a chance to escape.

That had been his childhood fantasy, hadn't it? Childhood and adulthood fantasy, truth be told. But again, Alan's words rang true – without Glen, there would be no Project. Would dying to save Connie be a noble sacrifice, or just an escape? Glen's pain and guilt had driven him to start the Constance Salvatore Project. The Project had, in turn, saved countless lives. If Glen died saving Connie, that would never happen. Even if, by some miracle, they both survived, the Project would never come into being. Without the pain of Connie's death, Glen would not have had the relentless motivation to fight through all the obstacles and hardships of the Project's early years.

Maybe *that* had been the true selfless sacrifice, his living with all that guilt and pain, to accomplish this greater good. And he had already paid that price, hadn't he? Paid it in full and then some. And he had made promises. He had signed papers. The school in Oakville was expecting him in three weeks.

And Rochelle...His treatment of her had been truly reprehensible. She only wanted what every woman wants from her partner, to be loved and respected, to be treated as more important than any other person. She understood Glen's dedication to The Project. She understood his sorrow. But when she had suggested that Glen needed to move on, to allow his heart to heal so they could move forward together, he had made her feel heartless and selfish. He had a lot of making up to do.

And really, the whole idea that he could go back in

time and change anything in the past was truly ludicrous. What had even caused him to think it possible? The more he thought about it, the more confused he became. What exactly had happened last night? What *hadn't* happened was probably a better question. Glen had resigned as director of the Project – his lifelong passion. His best friend and long-time mentor admitted to having been a murderous drug dealer. Oh, and he also admitted to being the one who maimed Sophia by bouncing her off of a guard rail into a police cruiser. Alan proceeded to tell him a wild ghost story then handed him a creepy dagger and suggested he kill himself with it.

If that wasn't enough, Glen had met an Egyptian antiques merchant who claimed to be some sort of celestial note-taker for God. An Egyptian who also happened to have both Alan's gun and Connie's silver cross – a neat trick in deed, since Alan's gun was last seen in the possession of his dead girl friend's ghost and Connie's cross was last seen in the possession of Connie's ghost. Not that that *means* anything. It certainly doesn't since there are no such things as ghosts.

Then what happened? He had come home to find his sister going Grand Mal in the middle of the kitchen floor, her boyfriend peeling out of the driveway – only to return a minute later. There had been ambulances and flashing lights. He had sat awake in this chair for hours. Eventually, he had fallen asleep in this chair, only to dream mixed and muddled memories for the rest of the night.

And now, the question of when the dreaming actually began seemed very relevant, and much more complex than it should have been. Did the dream start when he dozed in this chair, or had it began earlier in the night? Did any of that actually happen? *Of course it did, Glen,* he thought, *any hope of believing otherwise is just you trying to run away again.*

Sophia interrupted his thoughts. "Glen," she said in a hoarse, sleep-muddled voice.

He looked up from his hands. One of her blackening eyes opened just a sliver. "Hey, Soph, how you feeling?"

"How the fuck do you think I'm feeling? What a stupid question," she muttered. "And what're you doing in my bedroom? What'd you do, just sit there watching me all night? That's not fucking creepy." She rolled harshly away from him, the blankets catching and tangling with her jeans and flannel shirt. She sniffled, then yanked one arm free to wipe tears. When her hand touched the bruised patch under her eye, she nearly cried out in pain, but stifled it to a moan.

"Did Dale see the whole show?" she whimpered.

Glen put his hand on her arm and squeezed.

"Dale's a good man, Soph. He, uh, he got a little freaked out at first, but he got his shit together pretty quick."

Sophia whimpered again.

"He called the paramedics, and held your hand until they got here," Glen said. "He really cares about you."

"Oh, God, the ambulance was here?" She sniffled and, gingerly, wiped at her eyes. "Now every fucking body in the neighborhood is going to be talking about the spaz on J street."

"Sophie..." Glen tried.

"I didn't piss myself, did I?"

"No."

"Well, thank the pope and all his cronies for small fucking favors," she said in her feeble, sardonic mumble. "I feel like I've got two six packs in my bladder now."

She thrashed her legs, kicking the tangle of covers down toward the foot of the bed. Glen stood and helped her with the sheet.

"Hey, listen, hold up a sec," he said, resting one hand on her shoulder. "You fell, last night, busted your nose and split your lip. We, uh, put some ice on it for you, but it still..."

"I look like a fucking horror show, is that what you're trying to tell me?"

"I just thought I should mention it before you saw the mirror," Glen said. "Here, let me help you up." He took hold of her wrist and reached to put his other hand under her arm.

Sophia suddenly lunged forward, shoving Glen with surprising force. "Get the fuck off of me!" she screamed. Her voice was raw and cracking, but not lacking at all for volume.

Glen back-pedaled two steps, tripped over his chair, and landed with his butt on the floor. Sophia rocked on her feet for a second, found her balance, then walked unsteadily into the bathroom and slammed the door.

Glen lay back on the floor and put his hands up to his hair. From inside the bathroom, Sophia said, "You know why I wanted to be a nurse? To take care of people. That's all I ever wanted. I even thought maybe I'd get better enough some day...but I guess that's not going to happen."

The toilet flushed.

"But you know what else isn't going to happen?" she continued. "I'm not going to sit in this fucking house for the rest of my life being taken care of by my hopeless brother and some cute but stupid hospital maintenance man. That's for damn sure."

"Soph, Dale is not stupid..."

"He's dating me, ain't he?" She opened the

bathroom door. Her bedroom was still shadowed by the draperies, but the bathroom light was bright. Sophia continued in a voice the wavered between anger and tears. "Look at this, you'd have to be pretty fucking stupid to want to wake up next to this every morning."

Her matted hair sprung out of her head in a medusaesque catastrophe, laying bare her scar. The livid purple line seemed to glow across her untanned forehead. Below this, red-purple blotches circled both eyes. The eyes themselves were bloodshot, and her upper lip had swollen to twice the size of her lower. It curled up and out until it almost touched the tip of her nose.

"Well, I guess he thinks your other qualities make up for the nightmare that is your face." Glen sat up. "I tend to agree with him on that."

She wavered in the doorway for a moment, trying to decide how to respond. Glen saw her lips press together, which he hoped was her attempt to suppress her pathetically adorable wry grin. She flipped him the bird, which he also took as a good sign.

"What other qualities?" she asked. "I can't do the job I trained for. I can't remember shit."

"A bad memory can be a good quality in a girl, especially if the guy is stupid."

This time she didn't try to repress the grin. It made her face look even worse, but Glen was very happy to see it. He untangled himself from the chair and got his feet under him.

"You want some breakfast?" he asked.

Her smile died. Her voice was under control now, pleasant but very firm. "When I am ready for breakfast, I will make something myself. I want you moved out of that loft by the end of next week. You are not going to take care of me. You can't fix this," she said, pointing to the gash in her head. "And I refuse to be the excuse you use to stay here. Do you understand me?"

Glen nodded. He might try to fight this later, but now was not the time.

"That girl needs you. I will not be the reason you break her heart again," Sophia continued. "Oh, and speaking of Rochelle, she called our home phone for some reason, left a message for you."

"What?" Glen asked, caught off guard by the conversation's sudden change in direction.

"Yeah, she called last night. Anyway, I am going to take a shower. I know I'm not supposed to. If I seize up and die in there, so be it. You should be at work anyway, right?"

"I quit," Glen said, wondering why Rochelle had called the home phone instead of his cell. Wondering why she had called at all.

"For real?" she asked, suddenly more awake than she had been all morning. "You're not just jerking my chain?"

"No, not jerking your chain. I mailed Alan my letter and did a surprise announcement in front of everyone. I even introduced my replacement and had her give a speech at the gala. It's a done deal."

A true smile spread across Sophia's mangled lips. She took a couple steps closer to Glen. "That's really terrific. You so needed to do that, like five years ago." Just for an instant, she sounded like the girl Glen grew up with before her accident. Then, the instant was gone. "But that doesn't change the fact that you need to move out. Two weeks from now I'm changing the locks. Anything you leave behind I'm selling at a yard sale. Fair warning."

CHAPTER 22

GLEN CLOSED HER BEDROOM DOOR and walked into the kitchen. He had told Dale not to bother with the mess there, but apparently Dale ignored that suggestion. The beer cans and Jenga game were nowhere to be seen. The leftover pizza and salad were packed neatly into the fridge. He had even wiped up the smears and drips of blood.

Glen slumped into one of the kitchen chairs, disappointed. He had planned on cleaning up the kitchen. It would have been a simple time-consuming activity that would have required no thought, a diversion. Now, however, he had nothing to do but sit. Packing up his belongings in preparation for his move to Oakville really wouldn't be that much work, but just the thought of it seemed overwhelming. Maybe he should go up to his apartment and take a nap.

His eyes meandered over the various parts that made up Sophia's kitchen – blue curtains over the stainless steel sink, imitation granite countertop over honey maple cabinets, brass tone canisters for flour and sugar and whatnot, paper towel holder, telephone, answering machine...

Rochelle had left him a message, on this phone. He was surprised to feel his heart speed up. But why had she called this number instead of his cell? Maybe that wasn't as great a mystery as it seemed. Rochelle and Sophia had been friends since high school. She knew this phone number by heart. Glen's cell was a relatively new number. Rochelle had that number in her phone, but probably not memorized. Maybe she had lost her phone, or got a new phone but didn't transfer the data. Maybe she had called from a landline and didn't have his cell number handy.

Whatever the reason, she had called him. It meant the door was open. Maybe just a crack, but it was open. Having an open door when he got to Oakville would be good. It would be very good indeed.

He pushed play on the machine. It emitted a few crackling beeps, then Rochelle's sweet voice said, "Hey Sophie, Hi, it's me, Rochelle."

At the sound of her voice, something clicked inside Glen, a realization that she was the future, possibly *his* future. He could not pursue Rochelle and Connie at the same time because they lay in opposite directions. Connie, despite all she had meant to him, would be forever tied to the darkness of that night, all those years ago. Rochelle was optimism and laughter personified. She could be his path out of the darkness.

"I thought about what you said," the message continued, "and I guess you're right, I'll let him take me out to coffee, or, you know, something real casual like that...if he asks, but...well, I erased his number out of my contacts," she giggled, a little embarrassed. To him it sounded like the music of wind chimes singing softly in a lazy summer breeze. "so...could you ask him to call me, or send me his number? Okay? Okay, thanks babe, love ya." *Beep.*

Glen saw, in memory, the way she put her teeth over her lower lip as she said this last bit. This vision ignited a warm glow inside him he had forgotten he knew how to feel. Early winter sunshine streamed through the window, brightening and warming everything it touched. He thought this was an apt metaphor for Rochelle with her milky skin and fiery hair. Then he decided he was a complete sap and probably should get some sleep before he burst into tears with the sheer beauty of it all. When he got this tired, his brain tended to get mooshy, exaggerating every emotion to a caricature of itself.

He grinned in bemusement at himself and decided bed was the best plan for now. He would wait to hear the shower turn off – Sophia would be just fine, at least for this morning, and no doubt Dale would be by soon to watch out for her – then he'd head up to his room and snooze for a while. But later when he was rested, he would call Rochelle. Then he would commence on his life's new mission – winning back her heart. If he could make things right with Rochelle, that would fix things with Sophia...

Her words echoed in his mind, "You can't fix this." His head was too heavy, weary. No, he supposed he couldn't make everything better, but there was light ahead – hope – for all of them. He had known for months, maybe as long as two years, that it was time to move on. Alan had been his idol, his false god. Glen guessed he had known, at least on some level, that Alan was less than he pretended to be. He was, in fact, a fraud. Cutting all ties to him and to this place was exactly what he needed.

Glen yawned and stretched. He decided to start the coffee pot for Sophia while he waited. As he pushed his chair back, the shaft of sunlight struck its chrome steel leg. The leg was dotted with tiny droplets of blood Dale had missed in his clean up. Glen's memory wavered between two visions. In one, the blood sprayed through Sophia's clenched teeth, stippling the steel. In the other, Connie coughed bright foamy blood, spattering the iron rail as a eighty-thousand ton freight train bore down on her.

Bloody speckles glowed in the bright morning sun. Droplets burned like embers in the locomotive's glaring cyclopean headlight. And here were two paths, Glen realized. The Timeweaver's wager. One path meant his own certain death. The other offered bright sunshine, friendship, shared difficulties, shared joys and sorrows, beauty, love – in short, everything life was meant to be – everything he had ever wanted, for himself, for his sister. All it would cost was the life of one little girl. And she was already dead. So really, shouldn't he be free to pursue his life, to fix things with Rochelle and Sophia?

You can't fix this. He was staring at Sophia's blood, but only seeing Connie's. The price for his new life was more than just the *life* of one girl, wasn't it. It was the life of *his* girl, his first love, a girl who had fallen into the hands of those animals because she was coming to meet him, to get the kiss he had been too scared to give her earlier that night. And it wasn't just her life they took.

What exactly happened after Glen ran away? No one knew for sure, but the three of them had her in that tunnel under the tracks at sunset, and the train that killed her rolled past thirty-seven minutes after sunset. *Thirty-seven minutes*, it was a number Glen had tried hard to forget all these years, but still could not. She had been clothed when she died, but only with her outer garments. Her underwear was found some time later in the possession of a dead meth freak named Monty Goglioni.

Because of Glen's delay in reporting what he had seen, only a few pieces of forensic evidence were found at the crime scene. Among the debris under the viaduct, police discovered a railroad spike. It was coated in Connie's blood. That was another fact that refused to leave Glen's memory, no matter how badly he wished it would.

The sunlit path of love and happiness dimmed. Samir's words came back to him in stark, cold truth, "That knife is not a gift, it is a curse…as all who have owned it can attest." Whatever light awaited him in the years ahead, it would be darkened, poisoned by the fact that he had a second chance to save Connie but chose, instead, to let her suffer all the horrors of that night so that his own life could be beautiful. Only, it never could be beautiful, not really, not if he let that happen to her.

Glen stood, still staring at the blood speckled chair leg. He couldn't fix Sophia, and despite all his justifications and excuses, if he stayed, it would only make things worse for her. But he *could* fix what happened to Connie. *And what of all the lives you saved through The Project?* some inner voice, claiming to be the voice of reason, cried out. Glen decided not to engage the argument. Whatever benefit came from Connie's suffering, it could not justify allowing her to be gang raped and murdered. Glen felt his thoughts closing around this clarifying truth. He felt resolution wrap around his mind and cinch down.

As he turned toward his bedroom, and the knife, his cell phone rang. *Alan Fontain Home,* showed in the display window. Glen stared at the screen, bewildered, while the phone buzzed in his hand. When it stopped buzzing, Glen set it on the table and walked away.

CHAPTER 23

THE KNIFE WAS EXQUISITE, GLEN saw – now that he examined it in the full light of day – and designed with only one intent. Its blade was long and very thin, not designed for fighting or for any of the various tasks a knife might be put to. This blade had one purpose and one purpose only – to slip easily between two ribs and penetrate a heart. In the thirty-five hundred years since it had found its way into the hands of men, it had yet to fulfill that purpose.

Its handle, which had alarmed Glen when he first met this living relic, was indeed hideous, but in a way that fit with the blade's intent – many and various lives bound together in a single pursuit.

As Glen wrapped his fingers around this handle, his perceptions blurred, waivered. The memories of that night hammered his senses, rocked his consciousness. Glen staggered against the weight of them. The knife twitched in his hand, tugging its blade toward Glen's chest. He let it go where it wished.

The tip found its mark, just over his heart. A frantic, flailing part of his brain screamed wildly *what are you doing, what are you doing*...but that was the weaker part. Glen knelt, holding the knife in place with both hands. A new vision surfaced on the screen of his mind, the ancient Egyptian, Samir, looking up from his ledger. Disbelief and anger spread across his face, but below these two emotions, Glen thought he also saw relief.

The old scribe voiced a single word, "You?"

Glen answered, "Me, Samir. Start writing."

Glen pushed the blade into the meat that lay over his ribs. The pain was immediate, bright and hot. It forced all distraction from his mind. Somewhere else in the house, Sophia was asking what he had done with the god damn coffee filters, but this passed into and out of his awareness like a puff of breeze. His mind was on Connie, Connie's thoughts inside his head as he ran down the forest path to her house. He could almost see through her eyes as she ran to meet him. There was the gaping maw of the viaduct, and his sudden terror on her behalf drove him on.

Glen held the knife firmly in place over his heart and lurched forward, intending to fall upon the blade. But at the last second, as if of its own volition, his right arm shot out, catching his fall. *Even now,* he mused miserably, *as always, the coward*...The primal imperative holding him back now was the same instinct, Glen realized, that had seized control of him on a night so many years ago, causing him to abandon the girl he loved.

He tensed and trembled, knees and one hand on the floor, the other still holding the dagger's point to his ribs. A thin rivulet of blood snaked its way down the blade, over his hand, and dropped like ticking seconds into the thin rug.

He had spent years trying to learn how to forgive that fifteen-year-old boy who left Connie to die. And really hadn't that been the problem, all this time? An essential self-loathing that he exhausted himself trying to bury, but never really conquered? And the shovel he used to bury the hate, what had it been other than the oft repeated, angst choked, tearstained dirge-chorus of, "If only I had a second chance! I'd give my life to do it over!" But here he was, all these years later, after all those promises and pleas, the very thing he wished for firmly in his grasp, and yet still he faltered.

Downstairs a chair slid across the kitchen floor. A cabinet door slammed. Sophia yelled up the stairs, "Hey dipshit, you left your phone down here and your buddy Alan keeps calling." But that all happened in a different world, a world that almost no longer existed.

He found that tears were running down his cheeks, dripping into the carpet not quite as fast as the ticking drops of blood, but nearly so. The boy could be forgiven, Glen had accepted. He never had a chance of saving Connie, not really, and running for help – if that is what he had been running for – truly was the right thing to do. Yes, Glen decided, the boy *could* be forgiven...but not just yet. All those years of self-hate still had a purpose to serve, and he would use them to every advantage they offered.

There had been a span of months in which suicide had appealed to Glen. It was simple logic – he didn't deserve to live, he didn't want to live, why not just die? But he had rejected the notion as selfish and cowardly, the two defining attributes of his character he wished most to purge. Dumping his misery off on those who loved him did not feel like a road to redemption.

But now, that simple logic worked, *needed* to work, if he were to save Connie. He would need to sacrifice himself not once, but twice tonight. And what easier sacrifice is there than killing something you hate anyway.

Glen opened his mind, allowing it to fill with the images of that night. The knife thrummed in his hand as he did so, drawing details from the deeper recesses of his memory, thoughts he had picked up from Connie's mind, nightmare scenarios he had dreamed, the newspaper articles, the crime scene photos – he let them all flow through his head, taking every single horrible detail as an accusation, and accepting those accusations as true.

He bent his elbow, the one holding his torso off the ground, and lowered until the knife's hilt sunk into the spreading blood spot on the carpet. He had originally intended to drop onto the blade, slamming it home in one quick thrust. But a boy who would stand by and do nothing while his one true love is brutalized and murdered didn't deserve a quick death, did he? Glen thought not.

His elbow bent further, settling his bodyweight on the knife's pin-prick tip. The pain was excruciating. He felt the blade catch on the muscles and membranes between his chest wall and his heart, then pierce them with a gristly *crunch*. He felt the cold steel slide through the wall of his heart, felt that great thumping muscle beat against the knife's razor edge, shredding as it pounded, once, twice, three times, and no more.

He gagged, gasped, writhed for what felt like three lifetimes but in reality was less than thirty seconds. Then it was over.

CHAPTER 24

SWIRLING DARKNESS CRASHED AROUND HIM. The fifteen-year-old thought it was a sensation similar to plunging into cold water from a high rope swing. The older Glen had forgotten that experience, but understood the connection. He struggled against the swirling blackness, searching for a surface to swim toward. Bubbles of consciousness moved over his skin, through his clothes. He followed them upwards and caught the familiar memory of pounding feet, pounding heart, of the heavy forest scent with a hint of creosote. He grasped the awareness and forced his mind out of the swirl into the memory, which was no longer memory, but current reality. He was fifteen again. He was running, again, through the forest toward Connie's house, toward the fear and bliss of kissing her.

The boy Glen was oblivious to the presence of his older self. His hand still tingled in memory of holding Connie's. His lips tingled in anticipation of kissing hers, even as his guts clenched in fear of the same thing. He was terrified and thrilled to the point that he could no longer tell one emotion from the other.

The older Glen, though aware, was certainly not in control. The operation of two minds within the same brain was an experience entirely new to him. His head was above the water of consciousness, but he felt as if he were caught in the current of a high flooded river. He feared he would be dragged through what ever turbulence lay ahead, without the slightest chance of altering its course.

The rush was all-consuming, the rush of early teenage hormones, a body trying to shed the last remnants of adolescence, but not yet ready to handle the chemistry of young adulthood. His head blazed with all the varying stimuli – fear of rejection, desire for contact, real true love, awe of anticipation, awe of love returned, thrill of adventure, pure dorky amazement at the beauty of the world and all it contained.

The drives he felt were less emotion than instinct, a runaway train. Glen the younger laughed out loud for no reason whatsoever. Glen the older shuddered in terror. This boy was in the grips of motivation far too powerful for his young reason to direct or control. Whatever happened next was driven purely by the chemical mind.

The boy really *was* in love. He really was *in love*.

There was a whole world of things this boy knew nothing about – income tax and cell phones and terrorists and CGI movies – but there was one thing he knew with all his heart and what little reason he had left – the world with all its mysteries and terrors was nothing to him when contrasted with his girl. And whatever waited for him in the decades to come, he and Connie would face it together – they would hold each other together through the lows and lift each other higher through the highs and nothing could harm them as long as they had each other.

A horrible sickening grief struck Glen the older. Had all teenage lovers felt this way? What a ruthless cruel lie they had been fed. He felt a heart-wrenching sorrow at the purity and blissful ignorance of youth, followed by a dull red anger, an anger that bordered on fury. This boy, a boy whom he once had been, saw the world as it ought to be. Glen the older could not remember, at all, ever feeling this way. The light and the innocence that burned so bright in this boy, and in the girl who was even now rushing head long to her doom, were about to be snuffed out forever.

CHAPTER 25

THE RAISED TRAIN TRACKS FLASHED now and then through gaps in the trees, and the creosote smell of railway ties thickened. As he approached the moment he had lived his entire life to relive, the older Glen felt his consciousness ease into a more prominent place in this younger brain. The disorientation (which he realized was partly due to the fact that he now viewed the world from a set of eyes that were half a foot closer to the ground – and partly due to the fact that the brain his mind now occupied was flooded with teen hormones which tend to make any clear thought impossible) had eased, and he began to remember how to operate this younger body.

As they (the younger and the older) rounded the final corner, the older braced himself for what he knew they would find. There would be a moment at which Glen the younger would cave in to fear and loose his wits completely. Glen the older planned to step in at this point and seize control. It was a good plan. It would have worked just fine – except – there was one small detail older Glen had not remembered, a detail that obliterated his plan in the blink of an eye.

The viaduct loomed in front of them, an arched stone tunnel running under the raised railway. Three men stood just within its mouth, the trolls under the bridge. He heard their wicked cackling, but as he approached, they fell silent. The younger had every intention of walking straight through, he was on a mission. The older prepared to jump into the driver's seat as soon as the fifteen-year-old lost his wits, which would be only seconds from now.

One of the trolls, a tall sinewy fellow who looked like a young Peter Greene, stepped out of the viaduct's shadow. A cigarette dangled from one corner of his mouth. He had a black leather coat slung over one shoulder. After considering the approaching boy with a look of mild amusement, the troll dropped his coat over a fallen log and strode forward. He moved in a way that conveyed unearthly power, as if he were some minor god of all things sinister.

Fear constricted Glen's chest and throat. The older prepared to take control. Now was the moment he had been anticipating. As the troll spoke, the younger heard the words: "Beat it kid, go back the way you came," but the older was focused on the eyes, the melt-you-down-with-cold-fire, Roman emperor, fear proof, sky blue eyes…Alan Fontain's eyes. The face was slightly different – the nose a bit too big, a stitched cut under one eye – but it was Alan, without a doubt.

This hit the older Glen like a pry bar to the temple, and any hope of keeping his wits was lost. He swirled into the dark water again and watched – as if in a dream, as if disembodied – the younger Glen turn and walk back down the path toward home. He heard Monty Goglioni (known to his friends as 'Mogs') cry out when Connie stomped his toe. He heard the scream that had echoed in his memory for eight years, Connie calling his name, pleading his name. He watched the younger turn, only to find the troll standing over him with a knife. Mogs yelled from the tunnel, "Cut him up Carl!"

The boy ran.

The older fought for control, first of himself, then of the boy he once had been and now was again. The flood of confusion swept him away. He struggled for a hold or a grip, but the river bed was slick, and the current strong.

"Go back, damn you!"

"I'm going for help!"

"You're running away. Go back *now*, there's no time for help!"

"I'm going for help. I'm not running away!"

"The hell you're not. Go back, damn you!"

The older recognized the conversation. It was not he talking to the younger, but the younger talking to himself. The older had regained his own wits when he heard Connie's cry, but had lost all hope of gaining control of the younger. Yet, Connie was alive, which is what had brought him back to his senses. He had given up all that he was to be here at this moment, and somehow he *would* gain control. He had to.

He tried again to penetrate the panic in the boys mind, but it was like shouting over a waterfall, his voice was lost in the louder roar. The boy glanced over his shoulder as he ran through the woods. No one followed him, but he ran on, just the same. He turned back to the path only to realized he was no longer on it. It had turned, he had not.

This knowledge was gained in an instant and lost just as quickly. His foot went sideways on something in the underbrush and the boy flew headlong. The arms he threw out to catch his fall straddled the tree in front of him, but his forehead met it squarely.

The swirling blackness again, but this time for the younger. The fifteen-year-old had no experience with this darkness, nor had he any will to fight it. The older, however, was all will, and fight, and had grown somewhat accustom to this spinning inner night. The younger was gone, washed away in the dark river, and wouldn't be back for some time. Glen the older possessed the limp body that had been his so many years ago. He stood, zombie like, wavering for a moment. There was no grace or coordination in his movement at first, but as he limped back toward his destiny, he began to remember how to operate this smaller body.

Every beat of his heart was a hammer blow to his forehead. Each step with his left foot felt like all the tendons in that ankle would snap and his foot would fall off. He did not limp, however, nor favor the left foot at all. He actually stomped it harder than the other, reveling in the pain – partially because it forced him more to wakefulness, and partially to punish Glen the younger for leaving Connie to die. Maybe that was wrong, but just now, he didn't care. He still needed that self-hate to conquer the fear he was about to face. And, he wasn't planning to live through the night, so damage to this body was no longer his concern.

Night was falling faster than he had remembered. Enough light filtered through the canopy for Glen to stay on the path, but beyond that, darkness crept out of the woods and underbrush. As he approached the place where the path met the little stream, the railway bridge appeared through the trees.

The bridge, or viaduct as all the neighborhood kids called it, was a tall stone bulwark, holding up a bank of granite stones. The tracks ran east-west above it. The stream ran north-south below it, through a high, stone-lined archway. A footpath beside the stream formed a shortcut between the trailer courts that bordered the tracks on the south and the old subdivision homes beyond the woods to the north.

The evening sky faded from yellow to orange. Tree tops stood out as black silhouettes against this burning backdrop. The straight black border of the raised railroad tracks cut horizontally across the bottom of the sky. Below that line everything was black, except the tunnel's gaping mouth. This glowed with a muted mimicry of the sunset.

Glen alternated between trying to wrap his mind around the fact that Alan had been here this night – not only had he been here, he seemed to be their leader, the one calling the shots – and trying to put that out of his mind completely. It didn't matter that it had been Alan. It didn't matter who it had been. He was going to stop them. That was all that mattered.

That is what he fought to focus on. But how? How does a scrawny fifteen-year-old boy stop three armed trolls? He snatched a thick length of branch from the ground. If his adversary had been a dog or another boy his age, it would do just fine. Against these three, it might as well have been a pool noodle. *Maybe I've only got to get one of them,* he thought. *If I can brain one of the bastards, then take to my heels, maybe the other two will chase me and Connie can get away.*

He rounded the final corner before the viaduct. A large maple had fallen here several years ago. Its trunk lined the path on one side, almost all the way to the tunnel. Glen scrambled over this barrier then crouched on the other side. He scuttled along its length in a half squat, keeping his head down and moving as silently as his haste allowed. At the snapped off end of the log, where it met its rotting stump, he rose and peered over. From here, he could look along the stone wall that formed this end of the tunnel's opening.

The temperature dropped as the sun set. The air drifting out from the tunnel was pleasantly cool, but sweat ran down Glen's brow and cheeks. His heart pounded. The thugs who had killed Connie were no more than a stone's throw from where he crouched. He couldn't see them – they were just inside the opening – but he could hear their lewd taunting. Connie herself was right there, too, still alive and so far unharmed. He could hear her trying to scream through the hand that was clamped over her mouth.

His blood burned with adrenaline and anger. Boiled with it. He wanted to kill them all, not just bonk one and run. But this wasn't about him. This was about saving Connie, no matter what. He took three deep breaths, filling his lungs to capacity, charging his boiling blood with oxygen, then slipped out from behind the stump.

Just as he did so, Alan, or Peter Greene, or whoever the hell he was, stepped out of the tunnel. Glen froze, pretending to be nothing more than one shadow in a swarm of shadows. Alan's head was away from Glen as he called back over his shoulder, "Careful she don't bite you, Mogs. And keep your dick out of her until I get back, I gotta take a piss."

This was answered by a cackle and more rude banter, but Glen didn't hear it, something else had caught his attention. Alan's jacket hung from the nub of a broken tree where he had slung it, less than three feet from Glen's position. He froze, momentarily dumbfounded. *You ratted yourself out this time Alan,* he thought, then prayed desperately he was right.

The shadows had swallowed Alan, but Glen heard the distinct sounds – the fly of his jeans unzipping, followed by the patter of piss on dead leaves. Alan was maybe ten yards down the path to his right. Glen lifted the jacket from its branch. Its left side was much too heavy. He slipped his hand into the pocket on that side. A cold and deadly *hallelujah* sang through him as his fingers curled around the grip of Alan's .357 magnum. Had he been Glen the younger, even this may not have been enough, but the man Glen had logged several hundred hours as a firearms instructor with The

Project. He knew exactly what to do with this gun.

A scuffle broke out inside the viaduct. One of the trolls cried out, "Fuck! Fuckin' *bitch*!" This was followed by a loud, tooth jarring *SLAP*. Connie screamed, but the sound was cut off – probably by a hand over her mouth. One of the thugs roared laughter, cackling like a hyena on laughing gas. The stone tunnel's acoustics echoed and amplified the sound. The other one, the one Connie had bit or kicked, growled vulgar threats.

Glen moved quickly, covering the distance to the tunnel in three broad strides, keeping the gun low. He rounded the corner and plunged in to the tunnel. All that remained of the sun was a feeble reddish glow, but it was enough. The two shitheads had Connie against the wall, just to his left about five feet away. The one growling threats was behind her, trying to hold both her arms while keeping a hand over her mouth.

The cackling hyena had limp greasy hair. Colonies of infected tract marks crawled up the inside of his elbows. He had ripped Connie's blouse open and was now trying to cut her bra off with his switch blade. She writhed and flailed out at him with her feet. He danced away from each kick, then lunged in again, laughing wildly.

"Bite me again, bitch," the one holding her roared directly into her ear. He whipped his torso around, swinging her head into the concrete wall of the tunnel.

"Bite me again you fucking cunt. I fucking dare you." She went limp in his arms. Blood trickled from under her hairline.

This is what they did, Glen thought as he moved. *This is what I let them do.* There was no hesitation. He shouted "Hey!" The dancing hyena wheeled on him and set his feet. Glen's lips curled into a wicked smile – hyena's are much easier to shoot when they stop dancing. His hands and fingers worked as if this was the purpose for which they had been formed. Before another thought passed through either of their heads, Glen fired a slug through the middle of his sternum. The gun slammed backward in Glen's hands, its recoil a shockwave travelling through his palms, wrists, elbows and shoulders. Its thunder felt like open palms clapped over each of his ears. The hyena fell, collapsing in a lifeless heap. Glen shot it again.

The growler flung Connie to the ground and lurched at Glen. In the dying red light, his eyes were confused and scared, but intent on murder. Glen sidestepped his charge and fired, aiming to keep Connie out of the bullet's path. It was a tricky shot, and the placement was bad, shattering Growler's right collar bone but missing any vital organs. That was just fine with Glen. His mouth had gone from grin to smile to mad glaring snarl. The longer it took this troll to die, the more he would suffer.

Growler fell forward, trying to catch himself on his outstretched arms. His shattered shoulder tore itself apart under the impact of his fall. He collapsed in a shrieking, howling agony. Glen held the gun on the felled thug and scanned the tunnel for Alan. There was no one else here. No one waited in the gloom beyond the tunnel's opening.

The wailing thing on the floor got its one good arm under itself and started to rise. Beyond it, Connie lay unmoving on the ground, her dark hair plastered to the side of her head with blood. Glen ran forward and planted his hardest kick in the growler's gut. It flopped over onto its back with a hoarse wheeze. Glen strode forward and stomped down on its shattered shoulder, forcing another shriek from the wretched thing.

It grabbed Glen's ankle with its good hand, but there was no strength there. The shriek was replaced by gasping and sobbing. Then it tried to speak. Glen put the gun's muzzle on the bridge of its nose, waiting.

The thing said, "please..." then coughed.

Glen had dreamed this night nearly every night for eight years. That dream always ended the same way, Connie gagging on her own life's blood, choking to death on it, coughing that blood onto the iron rails above them until an eighty-thousand ton freight train tore her little body to bits.

"Don't you ask me for mercy," Glen said in a

trembling voice. He didn't know if he meant to fire, but the gun roared one more time, and the wretched wheezing beast on the ground silenced.

CHAPTER 26

GLEN RUSHED OVER AND KNELT beside Connie, laying his finger just under the corner of her jaw. Her pulse beat there, strong and fast. Endorphins and adrenaline flooded his reeling mind. His fear, though still present, had been eclipsed by a less familiar emotion. Connie was alive, pale and beautiful in the gathering dark. Two of her would-be murderers lay dead, by Glen's own hand. Had the third escaped? That didn't matter now. Glen supposed he should feel something about the killing he had done, but seeing Connie *alive*, feeling her blood pulsing beneath her skin, he could find nothing in his heart but joy and awe.

She stirred, opening her eyes. Glen's throat locked, as did his mind. What could he possibly say to her at this moment? As her eyes met his, something moved in the darkness. Glen caught it in his peripheral vision. There was a spark and a flash and a flame – a cigarette lighting. Alan stepped into the mouth of the tunnel, took a long drag on the cigarette, and leaned against the inside of the stone archway.

Glen raised the gun and stood. The sun was gone. Only a soft purple twilight seeped into the dark space below the railroad tracks. The glowing tip of Alan's cigarette illuminated his face, twinkled in his eyes. There was a power there Glen had never understood, a cold indifference. Those eyes said, "I can play chicken with Satan and not break a sweat." What Glen knew, that apparently Alan did not, was those eyes were lying.

Alan had been given the chance at a showdown with his own greatest demon, himself. He had stood toe to toe with himself, had seen himself for what he really was, and had run away screaming. He had, in fact, passed that responsibility off on Glen. That's what this was, Glen realized. Alan had not had the courage to face the mistakes of his past, so he sent Glen here instead, not to save Connie, but to stop his younger self.

Below him, Connie moaned and struggled to sit up. At the opening, Alan sucked on his cig, making the cherry flair. As it's red glow died, he called, "You gonna shoot me, or what?"

Glen scoffed, eyeing Alan over the magnum's front sight. Alan had known, all along. He had known who killed Connie, had known exactly how she died, had even known that Glen had been there and run away.

This whole time he had known. All his sympathy and wise counsel, it had been his own private joke. The man had to die.

Glen thumbed the hammer back, trembling slightly, either from rage or lingering fear or just plain exhaustion. He felt he should say something relevant, or profound, but nothing came to mind. Glen squeezed the trigger.

The dead *clack*, and the silence that followed, pounded Glen's ears harder than all of the previous percussions put together. At the end of the tunnel, the glowing tip of Alan's cigarette bobbed back and forth in an arc, forming a comic smile mid-air. He looked down, shaking his head slowly from side to side.

Glen pulled the trigger again, and again the gun clicked impotently.

Alan chuckled softly in the darkness. Gravel crunched under his black boots as he moved forward. "I get it, kid. I know what you're thinking," he said. "You're thinking you should have two more shots, huh? That's reasonable enough, I guess. I mean, it *is* a six shooter after all."

Glen could only make out his outline now, silhouetted against the moonlit forest behind him. He continued moving toward Glen in his casual stroll, a walk that proclaimed Alan owned every patch of dirt his foot fell upon, and every soul his eye touched.

"But here's what *I'm* thinking," his voice dropped a bit, the joviality slowly giving way to the bitter hate it had concealed. "I'm thinking those who need a gun to do their killing for them probably have no business killing anyone." A *snickt* echoed through the tunnel, the sound of a switchblade opening.

Glen tracked his movement more by his footfalls and glowing cigarette than by his outline. He was dismayed to discover that he was still pulling the trigger, again and again. "I won't let you kill her, not this time," he yelled. A slowly awakening younger part of himself wondered what he was talking about.

"Who the fuck are you, anyway?" Alan asked. "Certainly not that scared little shit I chased down the path. I saw the look in that kid's eyes, no way in hell he was coming back. And stop with the damn gun, already. It ain't gonna fire. I used those last two bullets on someone else, long time ago. Just drop it."

"Glen?" this was Connie's voice, tentative and confused, but lucid. Something shivered inside him, that voice had haunted him for the second half of his life. For the first half, her voice speaking his name had been an opiate no chemist could have matched.

And now here he was again, in this place with her. She was alive and he had a chance to keep it that way. He had come here tonight intending to die in sacrifice to save Connie. But now, having seen her, having touched her, having heard her voice again, he wanted to live, more than he ever had before. His prior life, he was beginning to realize, no longer existed. None of it did. Memories of that life were now only imaginings of a possible future, a future Glen swore would never be. She *would* live, Glen vowed, even if he had to die to make it so.

"It's okay, Connie," he whispered. "Get ready to run."

"Glen," she said again. She was getting to her feet, and as she did so, she reached out to him. At her touch, a weird vertigo rippled through him, his perception wavered. Glen felt certain he was about to lose himself somehow. Then he realized what had happened, Glen the younger had revived, was now awake and aware. The shock that shivered through him when Connie grasped his hand was simply the younger Glen thrilling to her touch.

"I don't know if I can run," she whispered, gingerly feeling her scalp.

"You're going to have to, Connie, he means to kill us," Glen said. He became aware of another change inside his mind, as Glen the younger came to full consciousness, Glen the older began to feel less real. His memories felt *thinner* somehow.

"Wait here," he whispered. "When I run, he'll chase me. As soon as he's clear of the viaduct, you run out the other side, got it? And don't stop no matter what. Don't stop running until you are inside my house with all the lights on and all the doors locked, you hear me?"

Her dark eyes were still vacant and dazed, but she nodded.

Alan had closed half the distance between them in his slow menacing saunter. Glen gently pushed Connie back toward the wall. Her blouse hung open, revealing a diagonal slice just below one cup of her bra. It wasn't deep, but seeing the thin line of blood there made Glen's own blood boil. He needed to draw Alan away, but what he really wanted to do was demonstrate some of his Aikido on the murderous thug, until there was nothing left but a red smudge in the dirt.

He would not risk Connie's life for his own revenge, and he had no idea how well this younger, slighter body could perform the techniques, but once Connie was safe, if the opportunity presented itself, he thought he'd like to find out. For now, he moved to the center of the tunnel, making sure Alan saw him clearly. Then he turned and ran.

Alan gave chase. Glen heard the boots echoing behind him. But just as Glen exited the far end of the viaduct, Alan stopped, then called out, "Hey, dickweed! I ain't falling for it."

Glen skidded to a stop and looked back. The

mouth of the tunnel was just a gaping black hole. He could see nothing inside. By the sound of Alan's voice, however, he guessed the man hadn't run very far past Connie.

"You killed two of my best buddies, asshole. By rights I should cut your guts out and string you up by them...and maybe I will, if you come back in here. But I'll make you an offer...a two for one type of thing. How 'bout you kill two of my friends and I kill one of your friends and we call it even? What do you say to that?"

Glen shivered in recognition. *I'll make you an offer*, was one of Alan's favorite phrases. He always used it just before gutting a business rival in some deal, or strong-arming his best go-to guy into staying with the Project one more season. Hearing that voice now, and that familiar turn of phrase, coming out of the dark maw of the viaduct played havoc with Glen's mind. The man who had held his hand through all the hard years, who had taught him how to be part of the world, that same man was the man who had killed Connie on this night's first iteration, and was now intent on doing it again.

Glen the younger had no understanding of his older self's dilemma. Hell, he barely understood that this harder, savage new voice in his head *was* his older self. But none of that mattered. What mattered was there was a madman with a knife in a dark hole with his girl and he had to do something about it.

Glen the older stood frozen in the moonlight, trying to think, trying to remember. Alan had told him where to find the gun. Had he said anything else that could save him now?

Then it came to him, not from the older's memory, but from the younger's. And when it came, it had a "duh! what kind of idiot are you anyway?" vibe to it. Glen had been a star little league pitcher – before this night changed him into something else – a fact the older had, until just now, almost completely forgotten.

"I'd say you're a narcissistic coward!" Glen shouted into the mouth of the tunnel. He raced forward, scooping up a chunk of granite as he ran. The weight was all wrong, but it was the approximate size of a baseball.

In the middle of the tunnel, Alan's Zippo flashed to life. It's orange flame glinted in his eyes and in his grinning teeth. He swung it in a slow arc, searching the dark for Connie. "Here pussy, pussy..."

This was a game to him. Despite his dead friends and the increasing likelihood that he would be captured or killed when the police finally arrive, (someone had to have heard those shots and screams) Alan was absolutely loving every minute of this. *Because he is winning,* Glen thought, *just like he always does.*

"Run, Connie!" Glen shouted, charging under the viaduct, closing to within throwing range.

Alan's light fell upon her. She crouched against the wall, holding her shirt closed with one hand and brandishing a rusty railroad spike with the other, her knuckles so white they glowed. Her teeth were bared in a rabid snarl that scared the shit out of younger Glen. It made older Glen's heart melt with pride at her bravery and made his blood boil against the trolls who had so brutally snuffed out that fire.

Alan's grin widened as he stepped toward her. He rolled the knife with his fingers, causing its narrow blade to wink in and out with the orange flame. Connie jumped and lunged at him with the spike. Alan parried it away with his left hand, dropping the lighter as he did so. It continued to burn on the floor of the tunnel. He feinted a knife thrust. As Connie moved to dodge the blade, he slapped her hard across the face with his left hand. Her head rocked back, struck the concrete wall. She collapsed in a pile at his feet.

Glen wound up and fired the stone just as Alan's slap connected. It flew true, drilling Alan behind his left ear. He screamed and staggered back a step, both hands flying up to his head. Glen hoped he had dropped the knife, but did not wait to find out. He sprinted forward, firing a second stone. This one caught Alan in the ribs, striking with a hollow thud. Glen scooped a third rock and continued to close the distance.

Alan was moving now, reeling a bit and trying to keep his feet under him. Glen thought one more rock to the head might knock all the fight out of him. But Alan's staggering and swaying made him harder to hit. *As long as I can keep him off balance* Glen thought, *as long as I can keep him away from my girl, every rock that hits him is bonus points. If it takes fifty stones, that's just fine by me.*

He hurled another, propelling it with not just the well trained arm of his younger self, but also with eight years worth of fermented anger. This rock glanced off Alan's shoulder, maybe a painful strike under other circumstances, but not enough to put him down.

Glen scooped another rock from the floor, yelling, "Run, Connie, run now! Go!" He couldn't see her, didn't know if she was conscious. Glen the younger noticed he could not hear her thoughts in his head as he often did. Whether this held any significance or not he did not know, but it wasn't a good sign.

He charged toward Alan, closing to less than twenty feet before flinging the stone. This missile, too, glanced off Alan's shoulder, and suddenly Glen's blood turned to ice in his veins. Alan was not reeling and staggering from a barrage of rocks. Maybe he had been at first, but what he did now was an act, a ruse to draw Glen closer and steal his advantage. And it had worked.

Glen skidded to a stop, preparing to bolt for the

far end of the tunnel again. He had lost track of Connie. Alan dropped his hands – Glen caught the glint of the blade in one as he did so – and stomped out the lighter. Darkness swallowed the tunnel, the sound of scrabbling feet filled it.

"Run, Connie!" he yelled, then bolted for the half circle of moon-lit sky at the far opening of the tunnel. Alan would follow this time. He could not allow Glen to fire rocks at him from distance. They both knew Glen would win that battle in three or four stones. And Glen had the distinct impression that Connie was no longer Alan's prize. His definition of winning now consisted of putting Glen in a hole.

"Let him try," Glen said to himself, and himself agreed. As long as he ran and Alan followed, Connie was safe. But where was he to run? As soon as the question was asked, two separate ideas fought for dominance in his head. The older Glen wanted to dart through the hole in the chain-link fence. In the younger's mind, the fence was not chain-link, it was wood – rotten red-painted clapboard at least twenty years old and fully engulfed in high brambles. A wave of bewildering disorientation washed through older Glen's mind. Where am I? How did I get here? The memories of the life he had lived after this night were fading, wavering in and out of existence.

He caught the understanding of this – you can't

remember something that never happened – but had no time to grasp the full implication. Nor did he have time to make it through the hole in whichever fence lined the tracks in this time. Alan was baring down on him. In three more breaths he'd catch Glen and plow him into the grit and gravel. Then he'd probably go to work on Glen with that knife like a Singer sewing machine.

"Trust me on this, buddy," Glen said to his younger self, and slowed his pace just a little, allowing a limp on his injured ankle. He was still moving pretty quick when Alan reached him, and Alan was at a full out sprint. He could feel Alan's breath on his back. The instant before Alan pounced, Glen planted his feet, dropped to the ground and curled into a ball. Alan had no chance to stop, his lower legs slammed into Glen. He sprawled face first, hands outstretched, across the gravely ground. The knife disappeared into the weeds.

Glen paid a price for his ploy. One of Alan's knees had struck him in the thigh, the other foot pounded into his shoulder. Charlie-horses throbbed through both muscles. As he staggered to his feet, he realized running again was out of the question. He frantically scanned the ground for a weapon, anything to give him an advantage. Railways are always littered with cast-off metal and wood debris. He just needed to find the right piece.

Alan popped up to his hands and knees, shaking

his head. Glen spotted an iron bar nestled in the weeds by Alan's back foot. It was about three feet long and an inch thick, the perfect tool for this job. He chucked a stone at Alan's head. It was a lame toss – his shoulder felt like a hunk of dead meat – but he hoped it would keep Alan down long enough for him to grab the bar and use it.

The rock clopped off the top back of Alan's head. He grunted, started to go down, but steadied and rose again. Glen grasped the bar with both hands and swung, pouring every ounce of his remaining energy into it, up over his head, and down at Alan's back. It would have been a bone shattering blow, enough to end any man or monster, except blackberry vines had twined around the end of the iron bar. They ripped free as Glen struck, but absorbed much of the energy he had intended for Alan.

The bar thudded against Alan's ribs, and the man who would someday have been Glen's best friend and mentor staggered under the blow. Glen swung the bar up again, preparing to finish the job, but as he did, Alan turned and hurled a chunk of granite at his head.

Glen snapped his head to the side, dodging the stone. But that movement, along with the swinging bar and his bad leg, threw him off balance. He stumbled backward. Alan sprung to his feet and charged. Glen tried to bring the bar around, but Alan was inside the swing of its arc. He fired an explosive uppercut into Glen's gut, sending the boy backward in a doubled-over heap.

The pain in his stomach felt all consuming. It sucked the air out of his lungs, sucked all focus from his mind. He knew what would happen next – Alan would run up and punt him in the guts. He didn't think he'd survive that blow. The gravel crunched with Alan's approach. Glen had managed to hang onto the bar. He now swung it in a low arc he hoped would intercept Alan's kick. He guessed well. The bar caught Alan across the shin, stopping the kick and drawing a howl of pain from its owner. The iron bounced out of Glen's hands and into the stones behind him.

He rolled toward it, jumped to his feet, collapsed under the weight of the crippling pain in his gut, then managed a slower, more careful rise. He came to his full height. Alan stood not five feet away, glaring at him. Glen saw, with some satisfaction, a thin line of blood trickling out of Alan's scalp behind one ear. The man stood crooked, panting, keeping all his weight on his left foot.

Glen risked a backwards glance at the viaduct, shouting, "Run, Connie!"

Alan rushed forward, unleashing a flurry of fists and knees and elbows. Glen deftly countered the barrage, his young body responding quickly to the older mind's years of training. Alan threw punch after punch, any one of which, if it hit its mark, would have drop the teenaged boy where he stood. Nearly every swing struck Glen, but most were glancing blows. The rest he deflected or absorbed with his hands and forearms.

With each passing second, he felt less and less like an adult, more and more like the boy he had been. Memories of adulthood slipped away, shredding like tattered clouds. They were no longer true. Everything that would happen from this point on was unwritten history, a history in which Connie didn't die under the wheels of a freight train.

"Run, Connie!" he screamed, startled by how little breath he had left.

Alan's attack continued, increasing in its intensity. Every missed swing, every blocked punch enraged him more, spurred him to further violence. Glen's battered arms grew heavier, sagging and slowing with each gasping breath.

Alan threw an overhand punch for his chin. Glen dodged backward, deflecting the punch down. The fist hit him in the sternum and sent him reeling, unable to gain his feet.

He landed on his butt, rolled away from Alan and hopped to his feet again. Black popcorn burst in his vision. He stumbled back a step, realizing just how badly hurt he was. Pain coursed through him in waves, buffeting his slowly spinning brain. This had to end soon. From the corner of his eye he saw movement in the tunnel, Connie was up and moving.

"Run!" he yelled.

Alan rushed forward, cocking his right fist. Glen had managed to stand, but his arms felt too heavy, too awkward. He could not seem to raise them. As he contemplated this, Alan fired a battering-ram punch, flattening Glen's nose.

The force reverberated from his face down his neck and spine all the way to his hip and knee joints, which when slack instantly. Glen toppled like a felled tree on the coarse stones. He could see nothing, nor could he move, though somehow he clung to consciousness. A billion nerve endings shot pain signals from all quarters, but the lines were down and the messages couldn't get through. *All circuits are busy now, please try your call again later.* The boy Glen almost chuckled at this thought, but the chuckle came out as a choked gurgle through the blood running down the back of his throat.

The distinction between the older and younger was now nearly imperceptible. The older knew he had had a life beyond this night, but remembered little of it. He felt a velvety darkness seeping into his mind like the blood that was even now seeping under his skin into the bruises on his face. The boy's mind caught, grasped the memory of that afternoon, of Connie on her front step as he left her unkissed, of her fawn eyes and her dark hair. *I'm sorry Connie. Run, please run, please God let her run.* As he thought them, these words mumbled through blood bubbles on his lips.

"Damn! Boy," Alan panted, staggering in exhaustion. "Damn," he breathed again.

It's over Connie, that's all I've got. You're on your own now. You have to run girl. He still could not see, but forced himself to remain awake. His hands twitched and flexed as he fought to revive himself. He could hear Alan walking more deliberately now, heard the clink and rattle of the iron bar as Alan picked it up. The man's boots crunched toward him across the gravel. *I'm sorry Connie, I love you...*

A new sound interrupted Glen's thoughts. At first it was a nearly sub-audible hum, or rumble. Alan heard it, too, and stopped. In the distance a low whistle howled.

"You're one hell of a scrapper, kid," Alan panted. "I probably would have liked you under other circumstances. But you shouldn't have shot Mogs." Glen heard him drop the bar to the ground, felt Alan grab the front of his shirt, felt himself being dragged up the embankment toward the tracks. He heard the train whistle again, closing fast. His hands fumbled for a stone as Alan dragged him upward. When he did manage to grasp one, his rubbery arm didn't have the strength to strike.

The corner of a wooden rail tie dug into his back. Alan lifted him up and over the tracks then dropped him onto the cold iron rails, rails that shook and rattled with the power of the on-rushing train.

Glen forced back the darkness just enough to open one swollen, bleeding eye. Alan stood over him, turned to head down the slope.

"Shari..." Glen croaked through the blood.

"What!" Alan whirled around.

"Shari sends her regards...from hell."

Alan grabbed his shirt again and lifted him until their noses almost touched. The blinding glare of the train's headlight accentuated his features in sharp contrasting white and shadow. He screamed into Glen's face, but his voice was lost in the screech of the train whistle. Glen grabbed Alan's shirt, dug his fingers deep into the fabric.

As the whistle died he said, "I beat you, Alan."

"You're already dead, you just don't know it yet," Alan yelled back.

"I was dead before I got here." Glen smiled a bright red, bloody smile, curling the fingers of his other hand into Alan's shirt. The train's thunder forced him to yell. "That's the train...Connie's not dead. I won! I beat you, Alan!" He spit a glob of blood into Alan's face.

Alan flung him onto the track. Glen's hands held fast and they both fell. The rails thrummed with the power of the on-rushing train. The scream of is whistle vibrated through Glen's ribs and teeth. The rails sang with the train's power – a squealy ringing like jingle bells, or styrofoam blocks being ground together. He felt them buzzing against his spine, felt that squealing inside his bones. The great creosote-soaked ties trembled, rattling the stones between them. Smaller pebbles bounced like popcorn kernels.

Then, over the roar of the locomotive and the rhythmic quaking of the rails, he heard another sound, a sick, wet thud of iron slamming into flesh and crushing bone. Alan's invincible blue eyes rolled up in his head, leaving only bloodshot whites. He fell sideways across the tracks, mouth gaping and closing like a clubbed salmon.

Something radiant and white stood over him, brandishing a gleaming sword, as if some Old Testament archangel, or perhaps a Valkyrie, had come to slay this demon. He stared at the angel, mesmerized. Then realized it was Connie, awash in the glare of the train's white light, the iron bar in her right hand still humming from impact.

She yelled something, but it was lost in the thunder. Glen pushed himself up with one trembling arm. Connie lunged at him, yanking him to the side. The locomotive exploded past them in a blast of wind and grit and screaming breaks, taking Alan with it. Together, Connie and Glen tumbled, slid, rolled, down the embankment, collapsing in a heap at the bottom.

For a long, long time they held each other and cried. The older Glen had nearly dissolved into nothingness, the distinction between the Glens gone. He held her as tight as his weary, battered arms would allow. Finally, when she stopped sobbing, when he felt he could speak, he said, "I told you to run."

"I love you, Glen," she cried softly. "I couldn't just leave you to die." She wept and buried her face in his shirt. The boy felt an odd sense of guilt deep in a corner of his mind, though he had no idea why. She trembled in his arms, he held her until she was still again. From that deep, fading corner of his memory came a final message, a distant whisper, *Kiss her, damn you.*

She looked up at him with her wet eyes as if she had heard it, too. He leaned in and touched his lips to hers – nothing more than a shy, fifteen-year-old kiss – but he swore to himself if he had to die five times, that one kiss would be worth it. She was kissing him back, and it didn't matter that their lips were covered in blood, nor that every single piece of his body felt mangled. In all his life he had never felt so brilliantly alive; and the boy had the strangest feeling that

EPILOGUE

THE NIGHT AT THE VIADUCT became the defining moment of that surreal and fragile summer for Glen, but not the defining moment of his life. This was due, in part, to the fractured and ethereal quality of his memories. When he thought back, more often than not, that night seemed more like a movie he had watched than an event he had participated in.

As the freight train ground to a halt, its locomotive coming to rest nearly a mile and a half down the track, Glen began slipping in and out of consciousness. From then on, only flashes of memory remained. His head in Connie's lap as men shouted and shone flashlights down on them from the tracks. Connie sitting on a gurney beside an ambulance, her dark eyes staring at him over her oxygen mask, indifferent to the EMT's poking at the gash on her scalp. The clash and clatter of his own gurney rolling into an ambulance. The soft beep beep beep of his heart monitor.

One of the odder memories was the fat police detective in a bad suit arguing with a nurse at his bedside. "Look, we got three dead needle freaks out there, one of 'em splattered damn near to the next county. This kid an' the girl are all we got for witnesses. It's a real clusterfuck."

The nurse's hand on his bedrail trembled, her knuckles white. Her voice was a whisper, but only due to her intense restraint. Glen could tell she wanted to scream. "I do not care. You will not speak to either of them until the doctor clears it! And you will mind your language around my brother, he's only fourteen, for Pete's sake!"

Glen had wanted to remind her he was fifteen now, but it just seemed like too much trouble. Then Sophia turned to look at him. Her hair was pulled back in a ponytail, exposing her smooth, lightly tanned forehead. The strangest thought hit him – her forehead was...*beautiful*. In the years that followed, whenever she wore her hair up, Glen remember that thought and wondered why he should have thought it.

Nightmares troubled Glen, troubled Connie too, as one might expect. But in addition to reliving the terror of that night, in opposition to those dreams in fact, Glen was haunted by a recurring dream in which he left

Connie to die. These dreams disturbed him far more than the others. He often woke with guilt stinking in his heart like terrible morning breath, and a vague curiosity as to just where he had found the courage to go back for her.

As the years passed, the trauma of that night – as it was first recorded and as it was revised – faded from Glen's mind almost completely. Sure, he could have told you, if you persisted in asking, that once he had been a boy who found a gun and used it to save Connie from a couple thugs, but he couldn't have told it with much detail. He let the particulars of his present life, and those of his more recent past, bury the older memories. The sharp edges and jagged lines of that night were lost to time, as terrifying and painful events ought to be.

There is one detail from that night he could describe to you, though he never would, for propriety's sake. Sometimes on summer nights, when pail moonlight falls through the window and splashes across their bed, he lies awake watching Connie breathe easily in her sleep. On the far side of town, a freight train rumbles through the night, its whistle echoing in the dark. Some think that whistle sounds lonesome, but for Glen it holds a different meaning. It calls fresh to his mind one of his fondest recollections, kissing Connie for the first time, both of their hearts thundering louder than the locomotive.

On nights like these, after the train has gone, Glen lies back against the pillow beside his wife, remembering how it felt to hold her then, how it felt to kiss her. He also remembers thinking that her kiss had somehow saved his life. He wonders why he should think such a thing, and is thankful he doesn't know.

Author's Note

Thank you so much for reading The Timeweaver's Wager. If you enjoyed this book and would like to hear about future new releases and special deals, please subscribe to my newsletter HERE. I only send out a few emails per year, and your information will never be shared.

I love hearing from my readers and welcome your feedback. If you enjoyed the story, please consider leaving a review on Amazon. You can contact me directly by email at axblackwell@gmail.com. You might also find me flinging inane comments into the twitterverse @axelblackwell or palling around with my writer buddies on Facebook.

Acknowledgments

This story was significantly improved by the insightful suggestions of my beta reader team, Michael Omar, CeeCee James, and Paul Deaver. I thank you guys, and if my readers knew how much better this story was due to your help, I'm sure they would thank you, too. Shayne Rutheford of Dark Moon Graphics also deserves a thank you for the excellent cover art on this book. She can be found www.darkmoongraphics.com

About the Author

Axel Blackwell is the author of Sisters of Sorrow, a YA dark fantasy novel. He lives with his wife and an assortment of animals in the Pacific Northwest.

Made in the USA
San Bernardino, CA
27 August 2016